"Tell me you aren't tempted."

His sweet adversary huffed. "Why are you doing this?"

"You're going to be here for several months. We should clear the air. Lay our cards on the table. Be straight with each other."

India stared at him. Her gaze was darker now, her face flushed again. "That's a terrible string of clichés."

"What can I say? You throw me off my game. Always have."

It was a bad idea to be having this conversation right now. The middle of the night was the witching hour. Defenses were down. Sleep beckoned. People made bad decisions in moments like these.

"You're intimating that you want me?" she said, her body language either wary or braced or both.

"I'm not *intimating* anything. I'm saying it flat out. I want you."

Dear Reader,

My husband and I live very close to Great Smoky Mountains National Park—which falls in both Tennessee and North Carolina. We hike there, look for wildflowers, spot bears and remind ourselves every year how lucky we are to have such a jewel in our backyard.

But if we had to pick another beloved place, it would undoubtedly be Wyoming, home to the Grand Tetons *and* Yellowstone. We've been to those two national parks multiple times, and the adventures never get old.

My very first Harlequin Desire was set in Wyoming, and now, some forty books later, I have returned to that iconic setting. There's something wild and untamed about the sparsely populated state—thus a fitting locale for an alpha *cowboy* hero.

I hope you enjoy reading India and Farris's story. They loved and lost and now maybe, just maybe, they will find their second chance in Wyoming.

If you can't hit the road this summer, head to your local library and do a little armchair travel. The wonders of Wyoming await you!

Thanks for reading...

Fondly,

Janice Maynard

JANICE MAYNARD

RETURN OF THE RANCHER

HARLEQUIN®
DESIRE™

Recycling programs
for this product may
not exist in your area.

ISBN-13: 978-1-335-73537-9

Return of the Rancher

Copyright © 2021 by Janice Maynard

This edition published by arrangement with Harlequin Books S.A.

For questions and comments about the quality of this book,
please contact us at CustomerService@Harlequin.com.

Harlequin Enterprises ULC
22 Adelaide St. West, 41st Floor
Toronto, Ontario M5H 4E3, Canada
www.Harlequin.com

Printed in U.S.A.

USA TODAY bestselling author **Janice Maynard** loved books and writing even as a child. After multiple rejections, she finally sold her first manuscript! Since then, she has written more than sixty books and novellas. Janice lives in Tennessee with her husband, Charles. They love hiking, traveling and family time.

You can connect with Janice at

www.janicemaynard.com,
www.Twitter.com/janicemaynard,
www.Facebook.com/janicemaynardauthor,
www.Facebook.com/janicesmaynard and
www.Instagram.com/therealjanicemaynard.

Books by Janice Maynard

Harlequin Desire

Return of the Rancher

Southern Secrets

Blame It On Christmas
A Contract Seduction
Bombshell for the Black Sheep

The Men of Stone River

After Hours Seduction
Upstairs Downstairs Temptation
Secrets of a Playboy

Visit her Author Profile page at Harlequin.com,
or janicemaynard.com, for more titles.

You can also find Janice Maynard on Facebook,
along with other Harlequin Desire authors,
at Facebook.com/harlequindesireauthors!

For Charles,
my favorite travel companion.
The best is yet to come!

One

Was it possible to go home to a place where you had never really belonged?

India Lamont gathered her oversize purse and her carry-on and stepped out of the small turboprop plane into the raw early-January wind. Jackson Hole/JAC was the only commercial airport in the country located inside a national park. Immediately, the jagged snow-covered peaks of the Grand Tetons captured her attention, looming large over the modest facility. The mountains demanded respect.

Much like the man India had come here to meet, the Wyoming range was sharp, forbidding, dangerous.

She pulled the sides of her coat around her and descended the steps onto the tarmac. Today, she had flown from LaGuardia to Atlanta to Salt Lake City and, finally, to Jackson Hole. She was tired and anxious and not at all sure she was doing the right thing.

Farris had wanted her to come straight to the house. India had demurred. She was booked into a room at the Wort Hotel for two nights. She had insisted this initial meeting be on neutral ground. If Farris understood her motives, he didn't let on. His texts had been curt and to the point. He would meet her for breakfast at nine the following morning.

India was relying on the presence of other diners to keep the situation from escalating. Her ex-husband was forceful and quite accustomed to getting his own way. But India wouldn't be pressured. She had questions, and she wanted to test his mood before committing to a plan that would put her under his roof for at least three months.

Riding the shuttle from the airport to the town of Jackson was a necessary evil. The airport was ten miles north, just off the highway that led to Yellowstone National Park. On a sunny summer day, the drive was postcard worthy. Today, the low clouds and spritzes of snow painted the landscape in ominous monochrome shadows.

India wrestled her large suitcase and two smaller items up the bus steps, stowed them and settled into her seat with a sigh. If she had agreed to Farris's preferred plan, a private car would have picked her up at the airport. She had declined.

When she finally reached the lobby of her hotel, the gorgeous holiday decorations were in direct counterpoint to her mood. Two employees were in the process of taking them down. Christmas was over. Now everyone idled in that depressing period after the January 1 festivities.

While other people were preparing resolutions to improve their health and businesses and relationships, India was about to take a step that might destroy her. This wasn't the way she wanted to start a new year.

She checked in at the front desk, mildly disconcerted to discover that she had received a complimentary upgrade to a suite. Was that Farris's doing, or was she being paranoid? Minutes later, the bellman opened the door to 106B, deposited her bags and accepted her tip with a nod.

After that, India was alone with her thoughts.

Her phone was still on airplane mode, by design. Now, reluctantly, she changed the setting and winced at the series of text dings that came rolling in. Her best friend, Nancy, wanted to know if she had arrived safely. India sent an affirmative reply.

Four of the texts were from Farris. Demanding information. Sounding autocratic even at a distance. She decided to ignore those, but then realized that he would only keep texting. Instead of answering the barrage of questions, she sent back a simple reply: I'll meet you tomorrow morning at nine in the hotel dining room.

She could almost see him grinding his teeth, his jaw firming like concrete, his blue eyes flashing with displeasure.

That was too damn bad. She was free of his spell.

As she unpacked the few things she would need for the night, it was impossible to shut off the stream of memories. She and Farris had been lovers for six months, husband and wife for barely three years and, most recently, divorced for half a decade.

Her life was her own now. She had moved on. Farris was merely a youthful mistake.

Beneath the stinging spray of a hot shower, there was no one to see if her wet cheeks were covered as much in salty tears as in water. She could tell herself the misery and grief were far in the past. But her heart knew the truth.

She was still vulnerable where Farris Quinn was concerned. Terribly so. The trick would be in not letting him know. If he sensed any weakness in her at all, he would exploit it. That was how he had amassed a fortune on the stock exchange. It was how he gobbled up small businesses like candy. It was how he operated. Period.

When she was dry and blessedly warm, tucked beneath the covers of a remarkably comfortable bed, she yawned and reached for calm. Tomorrow would be a difficult day. She would either end up going home with Farris, or she would find herself boarding a plane to make the journey back to New York.

When she turned out the lights, the questions mocked her. She told herself she had a choice. No one could force her to stay.

That internal reassurance was no reassurance at all.

The following morning, India applied mascara with a shaking hand. Hazel eyes stared back at her from the mirror. Her cheeks were pale. Dark smudges beneath her lower lashes attested to her sleepless night. She seldom wore much makeup, but today she erred on the side of self-preservation. She wouldn't dare let Farris know she was upset.

Her blond hair was chin length now. Farris had liked it long, so to spite a man who would never see the result, she had spent the last five years cutting it off. As an act of defiance? Who knew?

There was only one reason she had come this far. Dottie. Dorothy Quinn. Farris's mother. Dottie had been a source of comfort during India's marriage to Farris. To honor that relationship, India had come at Farris's request. To hear what he had to say. Dottie was ill. She needed company.

Whether or not India could or would stay remained to be seen. A lot depended on this face-to-face conversation with her ex.

She paused in the hallway just outside the dining room and steadied her breathing. No one waited here. When she peeked around the corner, all her available oxygen evaporated. Farris was already seated.

From this vantage point, his features were in profile—classic and handsome, except for the bump on the bridge of his nose. Dottie told India once upon a time that Farris brawled a lot as a boy. He'd been small for his age, and he'd made up for it by taking the world on his chin.

By the time Farris Quinn was a grown man, his aggressive nature was ingrained. Nothing and no one made him back down.

India grimaced when she realized her former husband was not alone. His mother sat with him. If he thought that would settle the matter, he was wrong. India would not be emotionally blackmailed.

When she had her smile firmly in place, she entered the room, spoke to the young man at the host stand and was escorted to a table for four. Since there were only three of them, she settled her large tote on the extra chair.

Dorothy Quinn jumped to her feet and folded India in a tight hug. "I'm so glad to see you," she cried. Farris's mother was short and round. The warm greeting put a lump in India's throat. "Hello, Dottie," she said quietly, glancing at her adversary over the woman's head of gray curls.

Farris had stood in the same moment. His innate manners polished his rough edges. He watched the emotional reunion with a narrow-eyed sapphire gaze. Unsmiling. Remote. His glossy dark hair shone like the ravens who lived in the park.

When everyone was seated again, the waiter took their orders. Then Dottie scanned the room. "I need a quick trip to the ladies'. You two children catch up."

As soon as the woman was out of earshot, India went on the attack. "You told me your plan was a secret," she said, low-voiced. "This isn't fair. You're trying to box me into a corner, but it won't work. I can still choose to leave. Dottie will understand."

Farris lifted an eyebrow. "Will she?" he drawled. "Besides, this is not my fault. My mother saw a text on my phone yesterday. I had to tell her the truth. If you had called me as I asked when you landed, I could have given you a heads-up."

India didn't believe a single word of his bland explanation. "What exactly did you tell her?"

He shrugged. "That you were coming for a brief

visit. I figured it was up to you whether or not to break her heart."

His mocking taunt was designed to make India feel guilty. But she wouldn't be goaded. The stakes were too high.

Before the tense conversation could progress, Dottie returned, beaming. "Now, isn't this nice?"

Soon, the food arrived. Everyone dug in with enthusiasm, even India, despite her jangled nerves. Her connections yesterday had all been an hour or less, no time for a real meal. She had subsisted on peanuts and pretzels, and now she was starving.

Dottie's excited chatter filled any potential silences. India responded when necessary, but she used the time to study her two companions, especially Farris. She had expected him to look older. Maybe she had *hoped* he would be haggard and unattractive. India was twenty-nine, Farris eight years her senior.

Except for a couple of silver hairs at his temples, his presence was the same. Impossibly sexy and gorgeous. But closed off. Unreachable. Though perhaps Dottie didn't notice, India felt a wall of ice between her and the past.

Dottie was another matter. She was so palpably thrilled that India had come, her face was alight with happiness. Even so, India saw signs of poor health. Earlier, the older woman had come back from the bathroom out of breath. Her skin was sallow, her small hands puffy.

All India had been able to get out of Farris during their one brief phone conversation was that Dottie was seriously ill. India would have to press for more information.

In that moment, she knew she had to stay. Dottie was the closest thing to a mother India had known as an adult. Her own parents had been killed in a car crash when India was fifteen. A few years later, when India and Farris married, Dorothy Quinn's genuine joy in her new daughter-in-law had been a balm to India's lonely soul.

She reached across the table and took the other woman's hand, her decision made. "Dottie," she said. "Farris tells me he'll be traveling a lot during the next few months. He doesn't want you to feel lonely, and neither do I. So I'll be staying for a while, if that's okay with you."

Dottie gaped. Her gaze shot from India to her son and back again. "This isn't just a visit?"

India smiled gently. "No. I'm going to be underfoot all the time. Do you think you can handle it?"

The little joke fell flat. Dorothy's eyes filled with tears. She squeezed India's hand. "I would love that more than anything else in the world. But what about your job? Surely they can't be without you so long."

"Well..." India hesitated, aware that Farris was as interested in her answer as his mother. India's degree was in communications. When she and Farris had finally separated, she turned down any financial support. But she had allowed him to do one thing. He had asked a friend in New York to put a good word in for India at one of the TV networks in the city. She had started out on the graveyard shift, finishing her days as the on-air newsperson in the five to six a.m. slot.

It was a brutal schedule, but she had adjusted. Other opportunities came her way. Now she had more regular hours.

Her boss had been apoplectic when she told him she was probably going to need a leave of absence. Indefinitely. He had threatened and cajoled. But India stood firm, even knowing that her job would likely not be there when she came back.

Her absence might not hurt her career. She'd had other job offers in recent months. Whenever she eventually returned to New York, it might be time to try something new.

"I'm taking some time off," she said calmly, smiling at Dottie. "Work is work, but you're family."

Dottie took the explanation at face value. Farris, though, frowned, a crease between his eyebrows. India didn't know why he would be surprised. He had asked her to come. Maybe he thought she wouldn't stay or wouldn't stay for long.

His gaze was unreadable. "You're sure?"

India had known from the moment she saw Dottie sitting at the table that she couldn't turn her back on the situation, even if Dottie *was* related to Farris. "I'm sure."

They finished their meal, though India had a sinking feeling in her stomach. She had imagined quizzing Farris and then taking twenty-four hours to think it over. Instead, he had forced her hand. Whether intentionally or not, it didn't matter. Dottie needed her. India would stay. For now.

After paying the check, Farris stood. "Mother, why don't you go up to the room with India and help her gather her things?" He glanced at India. "I had to park several blocks away. I'll move the car to the front portico and pick you up there."

"Of course."

Dottie chattered in the elevator and in India's room. Fortunately, it was a stream-of-consciousness conversation that demanded little from India, who was easily able to collect the few items she had spread about the room. Then she contacted the front desk. After snapping shut her suitcase, she took it and her carry-on and slung her purse over her shoulder. "All set," she said. "I've canceled my second night, and I did checkout over the phone. So we can head for the car."

Farris was waiting when they got downstairs. He took India's bags and placed them in the trunk of a late-model Mercedes. "Where's the pickup truck?" she asked, tongue in cheek. The Farris she knew enjoyed ranging around the ranch on horseback or—when the situation demanded it—a huge mud-covered Bronco with a V6 engine.

It used to shock her in the early days to see the suave, sophisticated businessman morph into a cowboy. In time, she had come to realize that Farris was both men. He wasn't *playing* at either role. He had tried his hand at horse breeding and kept a modest herd of cattle. Sometimes, she thought he was happiest here in Wyoming.

Just not with her.

She had planned to explore the quaint town of Jackson this afternoon. She remembered it fondly. But now they were headed north and east to the ranch, Aspenglow. Farris had purchased the property in the first year of their marriage. An aging Hollywood film star had put the place up for sale, and because Farris had a Jackson Realtor on speed dial, he had been able to snap it up before anyone else had a chance.

It had meant paying 10 percent over the asking price, but Farris didn't blink an eye. When he wanted something, he made it happen.

The ranch stretched for miles. Everything had been updated, from split-rail fencing to manicured gravel-and-dirt roads to the magnificent ranch house that sprawled on a narrow ridge like it had been lifted up from the earth itself. Built of timber and stone, glass and copper guttering, the eight-thousand-square-foot structure with huge windows that faced the Tetons was a spectacular masterpiece.

Yet inside, the house was homey and warm, though sophisticated.

When her marriage ended, India had grieved leaving this place almost as much as losing her husband and her mother-in-law. Now, stepping through the double front doors once again brought a sudden, breath-stealing surge of pain.

Once upon a time, this had been her home. Now she was an outsider, a visitor. She hadn't expected it to hurt so much.

Dottie gave her little time to dwell on *feelings*. "We'll put you in the blue room at the front of the house, near the master suite."

Out of the corner of her eye, India saw Farris flinch and freeze. "Mother," he said, "the guest room with the king bed is much larger."

His diminutive parent waved a dismissive hand. "But there's no view, my sweet boy."

My sweet boy? Even battling a host of troubling emotions, India wanted to grin. Instead, she kept her expression sober. "I'll be happy wherever you decide," she said.

It was no secret why Farris was displeased. For once, India agreed with him. The lovely blue room was far too close to the master suite and the bed India and Farris had shared. She would have welcomed more distance from the man of the house, but she couldn't protest without him knowing that his presence and the memories still affected her far more strongly than they should.

Once Farris deposited India's bags in her new room, he disappeared, leaving the two women to chat as India unpacked and stowed her belongings in a lovely antique oak armoire. The matching chest was larger than she needed at the moment. She had brought only the basics, not at all sure she was going to stay.

Now, with the die cast, she would have to ask Nancy to go to her apartment and pack a box or two to send cross-country. India had brought only a few winter essentials. Clearly, she would need more. And if she stayed until spring, then—

She shut down that line of thought abruptly. If she was to survive this visit, she would have to live in the moment. No looking back. No looking forward. Her job was to make Dottie feel comfortable, safe and happy.

Her mother-in-law sat down in the beautiful rocker that matched the other furniture. Her smile was pensive. "Have you been happy in New York, India?"

The question took India by surprise. It was no secret that Dottie had been devastated when her son and India divorced. What was she after?

India summoned a smile. "Of course I am." Present tense. This visit wasn't permanent. "I grew up in Jersey. For a kid like me, to have an apartment in New York and a job at a major network is the stuff of dreams."

"I've watched your show online a time or two," Dottie said. "You're very good."

"Thank you."

Silence fell, awkward…heavy.

Dottie sighed. "When I heard you might be coming to visit, I was hoping you and Farris could—"

India held up her hand, stopping whatever her ex-mother-in-law had been about to say. "No, Dorothy. Don't go there. I mean it. I'm here for *you*. Please don't see this as anything else. Farris is going to be traveling a lot, and he wanted you to have company."

"A babysitter," Dottie said sadly.

"Not at all," India lied. "But you know how Wyoming can be in the winter. Cold and dark and lonely. The weather can turn deadly. He doesn't want to have to worry about you." India paused and wrapped her arms around her waist, suddenly depressed and second-guessing her choices. "I know Farris and I disappointed you, Dottie, when we divorced. But nothing has changed in the meantime. Nothing at all. What if you and I have a wonderful few weeks together and try not to think about anything else? Can you do that?"

Dottie scrunched up her nose as if she had detected a bad smell. "Fine," she huffed. "No romance. I get it."

The touch of humor was welcome. India went to her and hugged her tightly. "I love you, Dorothy Quinn. And I've missed you terribly."

"I love you, too, daughter."

India's eyes stung with emotion. "Shall we go for a walk? The sun is peeking out."

Suddenly, Dottie looked older than her years. It was as if she'd aged right before India's eyes. "It's time for my nap," she said, the words wispy and breathless. "I'll see you at dinner, my dear."

India found herself unexpectedly alone, feeling as if she had failed in her task before she had even begun. She needed to talk to Farris, sooner rather than later. But she didn't have the nerve to seek him out. He seemed like a stranger now, his demeanor more remote and cold than ever. If the two of them were to care for Dottie in tandem, they had to come to some kind of understanding.

It was one thing to tell Farris's mother not to hope for a reconciliation. But it was another thing entirely to expose Dottie to animosity between her son and the woman he no longer loved.

India sat down on the bed abruptly, her knees weak. It was impossible not to remember the months she had lived here. In the beginning, she and Farris had still been in the honeymoon phase, unable to keep their hands off each other.

The rift had happened gradually. He traveled a lot. That was no surprise to India. She had known when she married him that he was a type A, ambitious man. But slowly, when he came home in between trips, he changed.

Instead of making love to her several times a night, he pleaded exhaustion. Their lovemaking went from creative and often, to once a month in the missionary position. Eventually, Farris began sleeping most nights in his office.

When she tried to talk to him about it, he shut down like the proverbial clamshell. Even now the memory of his stoic attitude had the power to hurt her.

She had agonized for weeks, trying to understand what she had done to push him away. On the face of it, she had been the perfect wife…following him cross-country to build a new life. When they were dating, they had often talked about having kids. But after the first few months in Wyoming, Farris claimed he didn't want to rush into fatherhood. He wanted India to himself. He used protection every single time, even when she hinted that she wouldn't mind getting pregnant.

His business trips stretched longer and longer. India was left alone for weeks at a time with no job, no husband and no friends.

Finally, the marriage imploded. After a series of frustrating, one-sided fights where India pleaded for answers, and Farris offered no defense, no explanation, she'd had enough.

When she threatened to leave him, he had been white-faced, but calm. In the end, India flew back to the East Coast, heartbroken and confused. Farris no longer needed or loved her. His change of heart was inexplicable.

Now she was back…and she had no idea how she was going to manage. They had been apart for five years. Legally divorced. The relationship definitively over.

Why, then, had her heart threatened to beat out of her chest when she'd seen him at the hotel? She didn't love him still. She didn't.

The only person in this house who needed India was Dottie. India would do her duty. It must have pained Farris to ask for help. He was a proud man.

India held all the cards.

Two

Dottie didn't come to the dinner table. When India stood to go in search of her, Farris shook his head, his expression bleak. "I'll check on her later. This isn't unusual."

India sat down reluctantly. "What's wrong with her, Farris? Tell me."

For the first time, his facade cracked. India saw a grief-stricken son. He stared at her, his jaw working. "She's in the final stages of congestive heart failure. The doctors give her six months to a year, maybe more, maybe less."

Tears rolled down India's cheeks. She swiped them away, her heart clenching. "Does she know?"

"I think so." He rotated his head on his neck, wincing when tight muscles protested. "I didn't catch the signs, and she never told me."

"How long has she been here with you?"

"Since Thanksgiving. Until this past fall, she and I spent most of our time in New York. My business is still there, of course. And you remember my mother's Park Avenue apartment. She loves Broadway and the museums, as always. But without me noticing, she began staying home more and more. When I asked if she would like to come here for the holidays this year, she said yes."

"How did you find out what was wrong with her?"

"Her physician is one of my best friends. One evening, I was telling him how worried I was about her, and he…well, he…"

"Breached doctor-patient confidentiality?"

"Yes. But don't think ill of him. My name is on all her paperwork. Technically, he wasn't terribly out of line."

"I'm glad he told you," India said. "Is there anything we can do for her?"

"Not really. My kitchen staff has guidelines about what foods to cook and not cook. There's the salt thing, of course. So the menu has adapted."

India was quiet for a moment. Farris had never been completely open and forthcoming about his feelings while they were married. But surely with his mother… She frowned. "Why haven't you just talked to her about it honestly?"

His jaw did that granite thing she hated. "Not all the world's problems can be solved with a conversation, India." The bite in the words told her to back off.

She inhaled sharply and reminded herself that arguing with Farris was not going to help Dottie. Before she could frame a response, the capable housekeeper brought in the first course of dinner. The woman was stout and pleasant, a native of the area. She was new apparently, not the same person India remembered from years ago.

India was glad. It was awkward enough that *Dottie* knew the history.

Over pan-seared native trout, spinach salad and fingerling potatoes, India tried valiantly to keep up the conversation. When she'd agreed to this arrangement, she'd never dreamed that she would find herself alone with her ex-husband.

Fortunately, Farris's employee was in and out, refilling wine and water glasses, bringing hot rolls, removing plates.

In between, Farris concentrated on his meal. He answered India's questions with the fewest words possible. Finally, she gave up.

How could she have done anything differently five years ago? She hadn't wanted the divorce. Her threat had been a last-ditch effort to get Farris to open up to her.

As a ploy, it had failed miserably.

She watched him out of the corner of her eye, her throat tight with regret. Again, the memories came in a flood, tightening her chest and stealing her appetite. She had been a very young twenty-one when she and Farris first met. India had been enjoying a warm spring afternoon with friends in Central Park.

Only weeks away from graduation at a nondescript community college, India had been a little anxious about her uncertain future, but on that particular day, she'd been having fun. Farris, the very serious businessman, was striding along the path, when India backed up and ran into him. The collision sent her feet out from under her. She hit the ground, winded. When Farris crouched over her, his expression concerned, she had felt a jolt of something far more than physical attraction.

That initial meeting turned into a series of dinners… fancy dinners—all at expensive New York restaurants. India's friends had urged caution, but it was far too late for common sense. India fell hard for Farris.

Honestly, she had assumed he was playing with her, amusing himself with her innocence and naivete. But he continued to ask her out, and she continued to say yes. During the summer, he complained when she took a minimum-wage job at a local ad agency. She was little more than a gofer, but it was her first grown-up employment, and she took it very seriously.

When Farris was free, he wanted her to be free, too. India, though, followed her own gut instincts. She might be poor compared to Farris Quinn, but she was not going to be seduced by his money.

It was three months before she slept with him. By Thanksgiving, he had proposed, and by Christmas, they were married.

Even now, she wondered why he had pursued her. That wasn't false modesty. She knew she was attractive, but Farris had power and money and a thoroughly male charisma that drew women wherever they went. He could have had his pick.

He chose India.

In his ridiculously sophisticated penthouse, she learned the meaning of passion. Farris was insatiable. He taught her things she had never imagined.

But a man and a woman couldn't have sex 24/7. Inevitably, his business demanded attention. There had been no mention of a honeymoon. India hadn't minded. Living in one of Manhattan's wealthiest zip codes and being spoiled by an incredibly sexy husband was more than a fantasy. It was her new life.

At Farris's insistence, India gave up her job. Not long after that, the Wyoming ranch came up for sale. Soon, they were on a plane headed west. They split their time between Jackson and New York.

India had been blissfully happy. The only thing that could have made her life any more wonderful was a baby. But she was patient. Perhaps Farris was right. They needed time to get to know each other, to learn how to be husband and wife.

Everything had been perfect until Farris began to pull away emotionally. Once, in desperation, India had even asked Dottie if her son had a mistress in Manhattan. Dottie's chortling laughter had convinced India her fears were unfounded, but *something* was wrong. That much was true. Unfortunately, India had lost control of the situation.

She felt her marriage unraveling, but she had been unable to stop the momentum.

"Would you like more wine?"

The prosaic question, uttered in a deep, masculine voice, disturbed her painful reminiscing. "Yes, thank you," she said. The words came out husky, almost hoarse. The pain was still there. Muted, of course, with the passage of time, but no less real.

As Farris lifted the bottle and poured, his hands were a thing of beauty. Long fingers, masculine grace. His tanned skin was sprinkled with dark hair. India had always thought a man's hands were one of the sexiest parts of his body.

Hands could caress a woman, comfort a hurting child, pen a letter or do manual labor if need be. India knew Farris worked hard when he was here at the ranch. She had often thought the physical exertion helped clear his head after the pressures of his life back in New York.

When he handed her the crystal goblet, she was careful not to let their hands touch. She couldn't bear it. Her nerves were shot, her emotions on edge.

Why had Farris not remarried? Sometimes she wished he had. Then she would have finally understood that she simply wasn't the right woman for him.

But he had remained single, his life a monastic one on the surface. When she combed the society tabloids for news of him, she often saw his picture at one charity gala or another. In every instance, he was either alone or had his mother on his arm.

What did it mean? The ambiguity made her restless. She wanted to have a huge lay-it-all-on-the-table confrontation.

That wasn't Farris's style, though. And besides, he hadn't summoned her here to rehash the past. His only focus was his mother.

The dinner wasn't over. There was still the dessert course to come. India couldn't bear the awkward silence any longer. "What do you expect from me?" she asked. "How am I supposed to care for Dottie?"

At long last, Farris looked at her, face-to-face, his gaze assessing, but oddly emotionless. "She needs company. Even when I am here, I'm often out on the property taking care of things, lining up work for my men. In the old days, my mother was never at a loss for something to do. She's one of the most self-sufficient women I know. But her life is different now. I want you to be with her as much as possible. Talk to her. Listen to her. Make her feel loved and appreciated. I do what I can, but I think she's looking forward to the idea of having another woman in the house."

"And what about you, Farris? Are *you* glad I'm here?"

Something flashed in his eyes, something dark and dangerous. "My wishes are immaterial," he said, the words blunt.

India flinched inwardly. Why had she asked the question? Why had she poked the beast? Was she really trying to make him crack? It hadn't worked half a decade ago, and it definitely wouldn't work now.

Farris Quinn had had five long years to seal up any weaknesses in his armor. He was an enigma wrapped in a puzzle. She would have described him as a stone-cold man, but she knew that wasn't accurate. The Farris she first fell in love with exhibited deep emotions. He was reserved—that much was true. But when they were alone together, he had been passionate, tender, playful and fun.

He cared deeply about injustice. He was a strict boss,

but incredibly fair. He rewarded hard work. He gave offenders a second chance, but rarely a third.

In his personal life, India had seen a side of Farris she suspected no one else did, save Dottie. He enjoyed giving presents. He had a wry sense of humor. And he was happiest spoiling the woman he loved.

Or he'd seemed to be.

Her eyes burned suddenly. As a young bride, she had found her happy-ever-after, but it had been snatched away from her. To this day, she didn't understand why. Not knowing had haunted her all the years since.

In the beginning, she'd had to heal. To remind herself that she was more than Farris's wife. Her personal growth had been a struggle. The eventual inner peace she'd claimed had been hard-won.

It wasn't entirely surprising that she'd had trouble trusting men. She dated occasionally, but in those early days, she hadn't let any man get too close. Her female friends enriched her life—high school chums, college buddies. And then there was her work family at the TV station. She loved them all.

She surrounded herself with good people, and she gave generously to those relationships. The lack of *actual* family members in her life was a pain she buried deep. No one knew how much she had lost.

And as for romance? Well, a girl could always get by with a vivid fantasy life and a few toys. At least that was what she told herself.

When the housekeeper brought in coffee and dessert, India was no longer hungry. She wanted to escape. But if she left the table in a snit, Farris might guess that her feelings were involved. Instead, she picked at her apple tart with a delicate silver spoon, taking only a bite or two as the minutes passed.

When Farris's plate was empty, she stood. "I'll check on your mother now. If she's hungry, I'll take a tray to her room. You can trust me, Farris."

He frowned, rising to his feet, as well, and rounding the table in her direction. "Don't you think I know that? I wouldn't have brought you here otherwise. I realize you're making a significant sacrifice, career wise, to do this. I plan to compensate you generously for your time and inconvenience."

It was a wonder India's head didn't explode. Fury rushed through her body, hot and cleansing. "Don't even think about it," she said tightly, wanting to throw something at his stupid face. "Dottie is *my* mother-in-law. I loved her then, and I do now. Nothing you can say or do changes that. She's my family."

"I merely meant—"

India cut him off with a chopping motion of her hands. "I'm not some tradesperson you can hire to swap out a microwave or paint a bedroom. I was your *wife*, Farris." She poked him in the chest with her forefinger. "It's as much my honor and duty to care for her as it is yours, damn it. Don't be so patronizing."

Though she wasn't exactly sure how it had happened, she and Farris were now standing toe to toe, breathing the same air. In the midst of her indignation, she realized something startling. Farris's pupils were dilating. His face and neck had flushed. His breathing quickened.

She wanted to take a step backward, but her feet were

glued to the floor. They were so close he could easily have kissed her. But why would he?

Farris didn't want her.

Swallowing hard, she bent her head, staring at his sock-clad feet. Earlier, he had worn cowboy boots, the real deal…the ones he used at the ranch. But of course he had discarded them in the mudroom. And since it was a simple family meal, he hadn't bothered with anything but thick wool socks.

"I'm sorry," she whispered. "Sorry I yelled at you."

The silence lasted for five seconds, then ten. Without warning, Farris put a finger beneath her chin and lifted it, forcing her to look at him. "I'm sorry I offended you," he said, his voice low and intense.

Gooseflesh covered her arms beneath her shirt and sweater. In storybooks, blue eyes were described as calm lakes and peaceful summer skies. Farris's had always burned with the color at the center of flames, hot and deadly.

But his expression was rueful. And still he held her chin.

"It's okay," she muttered. "My temper gets the best of me sometimes."

"I remember." A smile tipped his lips upward and put a crinkle at the corner of his eyes. "I've missed you, India."

He seemed almost startled when the words left his lips. It was her turn to flush. "I hope you've been well." She groaned inwardly. Her awkward response was embarrassing. This wasn't a Regency soiree.

Fortunately, Farris didn't seem to notice. He released

her chin at last and leaned a hip on the edge of the dining room table. He shrugged. "The business is fine."

"I meant *you*," she said. His words and tone troubled her.

"There is no *me* apart from work." His response was sarcastic, though the statement was directed inward, not at her.

"There once was." India didn't know why she was pushing him. Maybe a latent desire to hear the truth, even if it was painful.

Now his face was stoic again, all emotion tucked away. "You knew a different man, Inkie. He's long gone."

Farris really was off his game. She couldn't remember the last time he'd used the affectionate nickname. Had it just slipped out? He used to call her India Ink, or simply Inkie, when he teased her.

Their conversation had reached an impasse. "I should check on your mom…"

"Of course." His gaze was shuttered now, as cold as the winter sky. "Thank you for coming."

When India left the room, Farris realized his fingers hurt. He had braced his hands behind him when he leaned on the table. He had grasped the edge of the wood so hard his knuckles ached.

Now he flexed his fingers, feeling the blood rush painfully back into joint and sinew. How was he going to bear it? India. Here in his house.

The dinner he had eaten roiled in his stomach. His mother had worked three jobs to support herself and her young son when Farris's father abandoned them. Farris owed everything he was to Dorothy Quinn. He would take care of her, no matter what it cost him. Even if it meant seeing India and having to converse with her as if they were mere acquaintances.

He stared bleakly out the window, though there was nothing to see but darkness. He was the one who had ruined the marriage. Everything was his fault. Now it was time for his penance. He might ache, he might burn, he might crave…to no avail.

Nothing mattered now. Nothing but his mother's well-being.

He might as well get used to it.

India found Dottie still in bed but with the lights on. The older woman had propped herself against the headboard with a stack of pillows. When India tapped on the door and entered, Dottie was flipping through a fashion magazine.

Dottie smiled cheerily. "How was the meal, my dear?"

"Lonely without you," India said.

The other woman's face fell. "You didn't enjoy eating dinner with Farris?"

India stared at her. "I love you, Dottie, but if you keep pushing Farris at me, I'll have to leave. Dinner tonight was supposed to be the three of us. Your not being there made the meal very uncomfortable for me."

Dottie blanched. "Seriously?"

"Seriously." India sighed and perched on the foot of the bed. "Farris and I are *divorced*. Anything we had is in the past."

"But neither of you has moved on."

"Of course we have. I've dated. I'm sure Farris has."

"But you haven't remarried."

Farris's sweet mother was like a particularly stubborn dog with a bone. "Dottie…" India trailed off, not entirely sure what to say to convince her former mother-in-law that her efforts were in vain. "People who divorce are generally leery of jumping back into serious relationships too soon. I've met a couple of nice guys at work, but I'm enjoying being single and carefree for the moment."

Dottie stuck out her chin, the gesture oddly reminiscent of her son. "That divorce was nothing more than a piece of paper. When two people are meant to be together, nothing can break that bond."

India realized she was getting nowhere. "New subject," she said cheerfully. "I'm going to raid the kitchen on your behalf. Tell me what you want."

"I'm starving. Anything but asparagus, please."

"Coming right up." As she was leaving, India shot a teasing glance over her shoulder. "Next time, Dottie, come to dinner and you won't have to go hungry."

India was a little worried about running into Farris in the kitchen, but the high-tech room was dark. She rummaged in the refrigerator and found a plate of leftover baked chicken. She added two slices of sourdough from the pantry and a banana that was in pretty good shape. Dottie hadn't mentioned what she wanted to drink, so India grabbed a caffeine-free soft drink.

Before she could take a step, she remembered. *Salt.* Not a good idea. She grabbed a bottle of water instead.

On the way back down the hall, she peeked at Farris's

door. What did he do in the evenings? Work probably. She took one step toward the suite and listened. He loved music. It was a love they both shared. No sounds emanated from the master bedroom, but Farris was probably using earbuds.

India had stood at this exact spot thousands of times. This had been her space, her sanctuary. And she had shared it with the man who made her deliriously happy. She couldn't help but remember the first winter they had lived here.

She and Farris had gotten snowed in for almost a week. They hadn't been paying attention to the weather forecast, and the area had gotten clobbered overnight with two and a half feet of snow. The power went out. None of the staff had been able to get in.

The former owner of the ranch had used it primarily in the summertime. So there were no generators. Farris and India had survived on peanut butter and crackers and whatever they could find in the pantry. Weeks later, Farris had remedied the generator situation by hardwiring the entire house with the appropriate horsepower.

While parts of that experience had admittedly been uncomfortable, all India could remember was Farris. He had been so worried about her, so apologetic. Though it took some doing, she finally managed to convince him that she was having fun.

Fortunately, they did have an enormous supply of firewood, because Farris loved building fires in all seasons. The great room became their hangout. Farris kept the fire going, and the two of them made love on a faux bearskin rug with the flames blazing. They laughed and teased and worked together on their meager meals.

In a way, that experience had served as the honeymoon they never had. Just the two of them, drunk on love. Farris had been unable to work. No internet, no cell service.

Now, suddenly, the need to open that bedroom door swept over India with such force she actually trembled. What would Farris say if she walked in?

Five years had passed. She had found contentment and peace. Yet tonight, only steps away from the bed she had shared with her husband, she was no closer than ever before to understanding what had happened to her marriage.

Inside the master suite, a cell phone rang. India heard the low rumble of Farris's voice as he answered. Hot color flooded her face. Mortification swept through her body. What if he suddenly opened the door?

On unsteady feet, she walked rapidly to the other wing of the house. Dottie was already hungry. India had made her wait. Not okay.

If nothing else, India had to keep her emotions under control. She had traveled to Aspenglow at Farris Quinn's request. To be a companion to his ailing mother, a woman India loved dearly.

Nowhere in this unwritten contract did it mention lovers or romance or even closure. In her gut, she knew she should leave. Tomorrow. Before it was too late. She could take Dottie to New York…care for her there.

Even as the plan formed, she knew it was hopeless. Dottie wanted to be in Wyoming. And Farris wanted to be close to his mother.

All India could do was pretend Farris was no one to her. Just another man. Just another acquaintance. It would be difficult, because she was still attracted to him. Whatever curious magic had bound them that very first day in Central Park had survived intact, at least where India was concerned.

Perhaps she had inherited a snippet of her father's unfortunate gambling problem. Despite every bit of evidence that had suggested she and Farris weren't a good match, she had rolled the dice anyway.

And lost…

She should despise Farris for what he had done to their marriage…to her.

But that wasn't who she was as a person. She couldn't sustain such a level of hate and bitterness. Even as an orphaned teenager, she had known that her attitude would determine her future.

The truth was, she had moved on after the divorce. Her life was great. One day soon, she hoped to meet a man who wanted to build a home and a family with her. She was more open to the idea now, more ready to be vulnerable again. She believed the time would come, if she was patient.

Despite everything that had happened to her, she knew families were worth having. At their best, they cared for and supported each other. Even though her father had gambled away her security, and her onetime husband had nearly destroyed her with his cold, aloof cruelty, she had promised herself she would build something better, something lasting, something wonderful.

Sometimes the Fates demanded the scales be balanced. Dottie was a woman to whom India owed a debt of love. Because India understood that family devotion occasionally meant sacrifice, she would be the daughter and friend Dottie needed in these next weeks.

A divorce decree couldn't sever the tie between India and the mother figure she still loved.

Only one thing worried India. Did Farris somehow have an unbreakable hold on her heart? Was that why it was so shocking to see him again?

Three

India slept poorly. She tossed and turned for hours, stingingly aware that Farris was nearby. Without wanting to, she relived a montage of her marriage. Farris, naked and hungry, his sure hands roaming her body. Farris in bed with his computer, dealing with a last-minute crisis. India taunting him with a striptease to woo him away from his duties.

Even when she finally slept, she dreamed about him. His heated gaze locked on hers as he entered her. His silky black hair soft and tousled beneath her fingertips. As good as the sex had been, she had also loved *sleeping* with him, being held in his muscular arms, feeling as if nothing in the world could separate them.

Only sunrise dissipated the wistful fantasies.

When she finally climbed out of bed, she dressed

and made her way to the dining room at nine o'clock with a sheepish smile on her face for the two occupants already seated. Honestly, she hadn't expected to find anyone at all. It was late.

She sat down and grimaced. "Sorry. The time change messed me up."

Dottie passed her a plate of beautiful croissants and a butter dish. "No worries, dear India. I have the same problem when I first arrive."

Farris didn't say anything at all. He merely shot her a dark glance and returned his attention to reading the *Wall Street Journal*. On his tablet, of course. No one actually delivered to this remote location.

India knew she was blushing. Thankfully, there was no way he could see inside her head or know that she had dreamed about him being naked and making love to her. If she was lucky, he wouldn't notice her damp forehead or her quickened breathing.

The housekeeper came in and took India's request for scrambled eggs and hot tea. When it was just the three of them again, India smiled at Dottie. "What would you like to do today? It's pretty cold to be outside."

Dottie shuddered. "Indoors for me. Maybe by the fire." She glanced at her son. "I've told Farris I want to start working on photo albums. I've taken pictures and printed them out my whole life until about 2005. We had them shipped here back in November. I've kept them in the garage. But they're loose, not in any kind of order. I thought with you to help me, India, this might be the perfect winter activity. What do you think?"

Before India could answer, Farris lifted his head.

"Mother, it would be easier to scan them all in and make a digital album."

Dottie's face fell. "I don't like looking at pictures on my phone. I want a huge leather album I can hold in my hands and put on a shelf."

India felt caught. "Those big photo books can be very expensive, particularly if you have hundreds of photos."

Now Dottie grinned. "Money is no object. My dear boy has been investing for me ever since he learned how to buy stocks. I have more in the bank than I could ever need. Please, India, will you help me?"

Farris shrugged, his faint smile rueful. "You don't have any idea what you're getting yourself into, India. My mother has dozens of wonderful qualities, but organization isn't one of them."

When they all laughed, India felt a pinch of something in the vicinity of her heart. A mix of regret and sadness. For a brief period in time, when she was married, she had been part of a family again. After her father's betrayal and the subsequent deaths of her parents, she had been emotionally adrift—grieving the unimaginable loss that didn't have to happen.

Perhaps that was why she had felt so safe, so loved, when she met Farris. And surely that was why she had been afraid to ask questions when things began to unravel. She'd wanted to cling to the belief that she had found a forever home.

Tragically, the emotional safety had been an illusion. She cleared her throat, stirring her tea and not looking at either of the two who had been the dearest people in her life. "I think I can handle a few photographs. It will be fun, Dottie."

Her blithe assurance was put to the test that afternoon. During the morning, Dottie napped. India made sure Farris's workout room was empty and then did half an hour on the elliptical. After a light lunch, the two women met in the great room. Farris showed up moments later carrying a large box, the kind movers liked to use.

He set the first box on the round coffee table and went back to the garage for boxes two, three and four. He stretched his back after he set down the last one. "Well, that's it. Good luck, ladies."

India's eyes widened. Dottie had already ripped open the top of the first box. Judging by the contents India could see, the pictures might number in the *thousands*, not the hundreds. She chewed her lip, already pondering the logistics. "Are they at least grouped by years in the boxes?"

Dottie shook her head, her smile cheerful. "No. They were in a large chest of drawers. Whenever I picked them up at the drugstore, I would look at them and then put the envelope, negatives and all, in the bureau."

"Ah."

Farris didn't even bother to hide his amusement. "Good thing you're here for more than a short visit."

India gave him a withering look behind Dottie's back. "We can do this," she said to Dottie. "And I'm sure Farris might lend a hand now and then."

"Oh, no," he said. "I've got ranch work from dawn until dusk."

"And what about *after* dusk?" she asked, glaring at him.

He shrugged, trying and failing to look innocent and

regretful. "I keep up with the New York business in the evenings. No time for goofing off."

"Helping your sweet mother is *not* goofing off," India insisted.

For the first time since India had arrived, Farris smiled, a full-on, gorgeous flash of white teeth. "That's what I have you for, Inkie."

Three hours later, India arched her back and groaned. She and Dottie had bent over the coffee table nonstop, sifting through photographs and separating them into piles. Dottie was no help at all. Every third or fourth image prompted a story.

India sighed, holding out a handful of prints. "Dottie, you're going to have to get rid of a lot of these or we'll never get finished. This stack has sixteen almost-identical copies of bougainvillea from your trip to Hawaii in 2008. Pick the nicest one, and we'll toss the rest. Please."

Dottie took the pictures and flipped through them. "But they're all so good. Farris had just bought me a top-of-the-line digital camera for my birthday."

"And now a smartphone can do even better. What's the point, Dottie? You only need one. If you can't bear to throw them away, let me do it, and let's move on."

"Fine," Dottie huffed. "I pick this one." She laid the winner carefully on the table. "But I'm tired of this box. I'd rather look at some of the older stuff."

"Whatever you say." India took a pair of scissors and slit the tape on a box labeled *Early Years*. "Is this what you're looking for?"

Dottie reached in and took out an age-stained envelope. Her smile faded. "Yes. This one says 1988. I remember this batch." She took out the prints. "Look, India. This was Farris's first day of kindergarten. Or maybe first grade. I can't remember."

India took the photograph and studied it. The young boy was instantly recognizable. The same blue eyes, the same steady stare. "He looks sad," she said.

"His father had just abandoned us." Dottie's voice didn't wobble. She didn't blink or wince or give any indication at all that the memory upset her.

"I knew he left, but I never heard the whole story."

Dottie shrugged. "I discovered my husband had another family. One that predated me and my son."

India was stunned. This was huge. Why had Farris never told her about something so formative in his past? Surely this was the kind of traumatic experience that one spouse shared with another.

Had she ever known him at all?

"Oh, my God. I'm so sorry," she said.

"It was a long time ago. I got over the man, but I've never forgiven myself for harming my son."

"You didn't harm him. Farris turned into a wonderful, successful man."

"It took a long time." Dottie sat back on the sofa with a sigh. "My poor boy was so angry all the time. So hurt. How can a child understand what it took me years to deal with? Sometimes I think Farris will always bear those scars."

India didn't know what to say to that. It was true that Farris wasn't a warm, fuzzy man. But when he had wooed India, he had been irresistible. She had adored his infrequent smiles, his passionate lovemaking, his tender humor.

He had never talked to her about his childhood, not really. Bits and pieces here and there. She knew Dottie had been a single mother. But India had never asked about the details. Her yearning for a family had encouraged her to accept everything at face value. Now she had the maturity to realize that she had accepted far less than she deserved. And infinitely less than she wanted and needed. Her *perfect* marriage had been underpinned with too many secrets to survive.

Though India and Dottie had been on very good terms during the marriage, Dottie hadn't lived with Farris back then, of course. She'd had her own place and a full social life. India had seen her often, but never for huge blocks of time, not like now. There hadn't been the opportunity for deep heart-to-hearts.

Although, looking back, perhaps that wasn't exactly true. Maybe she and Dottie had honored an unspoken agreement not to delve too deeply into Farris's psyche or the Quinn family past.

When she glanced over at Dottie, she knew something was wrong. "Dottie," she said urgently. "Are you okay?"

Farris's mother was flushed. Her chest rose and fell rapidly with her harsh breathing. "I'm fine," she said.

India decided in an instant that she couldn't tiptoe around the subject for weeks on end. She sat beside Dottie and took her hand. "Farris told me you've been ill. I want to take care of you, but I need you to let me know when you need to rest."

Dottie closed her eyes and grimaced. "Bloody, stupid heart of mine. Don't get old, my sweet girl. It sucks."

India laughed softly, as Dottie had intended, but she was concerned. Dottie wasn't old at all. Barely sixty. India had read up on Dottie's condition since Farris told her the whole story. There were a multitude of possible causes. Unfortunately, at this late stage, there was no cure.

"Let me help you up." India took the older woman's hands and gently pulled her to her feet. "Can I get you anything?"

Dottie shook her head, her expression stubborn. "Nope. I want a nap. And I may watch TV in my room later."

India slipped an arm around her waist. "I'll walk with you," she said.

"Don't fuss, India. I'm fine." Dottie shrugged off the support and ambled slowly toward her room.

India stood in the foyer, watching until her charge disappeared from sight. How was this going to work? She couldn't be a caregiver if Dottie didn't want to have help.

Farris came around the corner from the direction of his room. "What's wrong?"

"I don't know. Your mother suddenly got tired and didn't want to work on the pictures anymore. But she wouldn't let me help her to her room."

Farris sighed. "That sounds about right. She can only exert herself to a certain point. Then she fades fast."

India shifted from one foot to the other, trying not to notice the way Farris's white button-down shirt left his throat bare. His hair was damp as if he had recently taken a shower. India remembered that bathroom well, even though it had been five years since she had seen it. An enormous shower enclosure. Dual rain heads. A heated floor. Built-in seats of smooth local granite. A detachable sprayer that could be used for all kinds of games.

Her breathing quickened, remembering in vivid detail the naughty sex play she and Farris had enjoyed. Today, he was wearing jeans, but the shirt could have paired nicely with a dark suit. Again, she was struck by the dichotomies in his personality.

Who was Farris Quinn? The cutthroat financier? Or the rugged cowboy?

She looked at him, trying to concentrate on her responsibilities. "Shouldn't I take Dottie back to New York and care for her there? If you're traveling, I don't know that I'll be comfortable looking after her here. We're so far from town. And does she even have a doctor at the Jackson hospital?"

Farris leaned against the wall and folded his arms across his chest. She saw worry in his gaze…and a certain fatalism. "What you say makes sense. But Dottie is worried about contagion. She says there are too many people in the city, too many germs. She feels safer here. The doctor actually told her *not* to get sick. Even a cold can tax her body."

"I see."

"Don't worry about her, India. My mother has made peace with whatever happens. And, honestly, she's not in imminent danger."

"But her condition could change rapidly, right? I did

some reading last night, trying to understand everything that's going on."

"It could. She could have a heart attack. Or a stroke. The more likely scenario is that she will gradually go downhill. I don't want you to feel responsible."

"How can I not?"

Farris straightened. "How about we go for a ride?"

Her heart bumped. "Isn't it cold?"

He shrugged and grinned. "Twenty-nine degrees. And the sun is shining. You can't stay cooped up in this house all day."

"But what about Dottie?"

"I'll text her, so I won't disturb her nap. She'll see it when she wakes up."

"Okay. I guess that would be fun."

"Meet me at the barn in fifteen minutes."

In the lovely blue guest suite, India rummaged in her suitcase for the appropriate clothing. An old, faded pair of jeans would do. And a warm red turtleneck sweater. Thick socks and ankle-high leather boots, and she was ready.

She glanced around the room. Already, she was fond of her new accommodations. It seemed odd that Dottie hadn't claimed this room-with-a-view. The house encompassed a single level with one wing like the base of a lazy backward L. The kitchen and great room/den occupied the central part of the structure. The master suite and the blue room were to the left. Dottie's quarters, a workout room and a second guest room were located in the section that angled back and to the right. If Farris was ever in residence on his own, there were large doors that made it possible to close off the section where Dottie now resided.

In the context of India's brief marriage, she had thought about children often. This amazing house would be a lovely spot to raise a family...for at least six months out of the year. And then New York for the rest. The best of both worlds.

For a brief moment, she couldn't help thinking about what she had lost. Not only her husband, but all the might-have-beens, as well.

Then she lifted her chin, though there was no one around to see the defiant gesture. She refused to dwell on the past. Her plans and dreams for the future were intact. Against all odds, she had created a good life for herself. A life that didn't include Farris, but a future that would almost assuredly bring her the family she so craved.

She would break the cycle of her aloneness. In fact, she'd already done that with her many wonderful friendships. It was time to find the man who would be the perfect husband and father.

After running a brush through her hair, she grabbed up her heavy coat. When she stepped outside, the cold slapped her, but not unpleasantly. More of a brisk wake-up call. The sunshine softened the brunt of the icy air.

She slipped on her gloves and pulled up her hood. Farris was in the barn, as promised. The smells of hay and leather and animals were pleasant. "I have to warn you," she said. "I haven't been on a horse in a very long time. I was thinking you should give me your dullest, slowest ride."

Farris was tightening the saddle on a huge, restless

black stallion, a flawless animal she didn't remember. He looked at India over his shoulder. "I thought you could ride behind me," he said.

Shocked, she searched his words for hidden meanings. His tone was neither teasing nor flirtatious. Apparently, he simply thought there was no problem with a formerly married couple riding together on one giant beast.

"Um, well…okay." She was dazed by the idea and couldn't come up with a suitable response.

Farris put one foot into the stirrup and elevated himself into the saddle with a smooth, natural movement that stole her breath. The man was born to ride a horse, all evidence to the contrary. He might have been only a boy from Jersey, but somewhere in his DNA, there must have been an equestrian or two.

To be honest, India was a little intimidated by the stallion. "Does he bite?" she asked, eyeing the animal with a mix of respect and dread.

"No." Farris chuckled. "Come on. We're wasting daylight." He reached down. "Take my hand. You've done this before."

Of course she had. Blindly, India tucked her fingers in his and let him pull her up. Her mounting was far less elegant, but she didn't fall off the other side.

Suddenly, she was pressed against her ex-husband's back, her legs spread wide on either side of his. For a few minutes, she forgot to breathe. He smelled delightful. Even through his clothing and hers, the heat of his body began to warm her.

"Where are we going?" she asked. The words ended on a squeak when, without warning, Farris jumped the horse over the corral fence. Her arms tightened around his waist. She was afraid to touch him, but even more afraid of tumbling to the ground.

"I want you to see the improvements," he said.

They galloped along the dirt-and-gravel road that cut through the center of the ranch. In the past, she had ridden with Farris most days. She had been a timid rider, but he had taught her the skills to feel comfortable in the saddle. He had even bought her a beautiful mare who was smaller and less threatening than the rest of his stable.

Now, with the wind whipping her cheeks and the open vistas stretching toward the magnificent Tetons in the distance, India was pummeled with emotions that threatened to shred her heart. Exhilaration. Joy. Regret. Pain.

She had walked away from all of this. But there had been no choice.

Farris slowed the horse and pointed to a small cluster of buildings. "I decided equine breeding wasn't the way I wanted to go. I've hired a ranch foreman, an assistant and five wranglers. We've built up the beef herd. The water here is pristine, and the grasses are protein rich. Slowly, we're building a reputation for Aspenglow beef. Soon, we'll be selling regularly to a dozen states."

"That's wonderful," India said. She studied the bunkhouse and what was probably a storage shed for additional tackle and tools. "What's that building?" It was obviously new. One level. Log construction.

"It's a duplex, or two apartments, you might say. A couple of my guys are married. They prefer to live onsite and cut out the commute."

"I can understand why." The open range rolled for miles in front of them, broken up only by small clumps of trees here and there and a narrow river. Back East, it would have been called a big creek, but that was the nature of water in a dry place like this.

They moved on. Farris showed her the central area where most of the cattle grazed. He indicated the array of solar panels that provided a growing percentage of the ranch's power needs.

It was clear to India that Aspenglow was no longer just a hobby for Farris. He had thrown his heart, his time and attention and a staggering amount of money into his Western adventure.

They dismounted at last near a single picnic table by the side of the river. Farris hopped down and then held up his arms to help India. His hands settled on her waist, steadying her as she slid off the animal. There was a moment when he supported her entire weight, their bodies brushing.

India couldn't look at his face. What was he thinking? To have him touch her, even in this context, shattered her composure. Because she was so rattled, she stepped away immediately when her feet were on solid ground. Staring at the river enabled her to ignore Farris and pull herself together.

The water looked cold. Crusts of ice along the edges attested to the overnight temperatures. The sound of the water was soothing.

The two of them sat on top of the table, their feet propped on the bench.

Farris gazed out over the land, his expression pensive. "Well, what do you think?"

Was he really asking her opinion? "It's amazing, Farris. So much more than the property you first acquired. You must be very proud."

"It feels good," he said. "Better than making digital money and putting it in virtual banks."

"But those digital investments gave you the financial freedom you needed to buy all of this, right?"

"I suppose." He seemed restless. The fingers of one hand drummed on his thigh.

She half turned, wanting to see his face. "Are you happy, Farris?"

He frowned. "What kind of question is that?"

"A serious one. I think of you often and hope that you've found contentment at least. I know the two of us weren't a good match. You were older and sophisticated. I was too young and naive. It was bound to end badly."

He responded with a scowl. "Don't be ridiculous. You were perfect."

She gaped at him. "We *divorced*, Farris. That's the opposite of perfection. Most people would call it a monumental failure."

"India. You know the breakup was my fault. I see no point in rehashing old history."

She stared at him blankly. Her brain was blank, as well. "Your fault?"

Farris jumped down from the table. "Come on," he said curtly. "It's getting dark."

He was right. The winter days were short. Soon, the sun would disappear behind the jagged peaks of the mountains in the distance.

Joining Farris on the horse this time was much

harder. Not the physical part. He brought the stallion to the table, so India was easily able to mount.

But sliding her arms around him felt unbearably intimate. Why had she ever agreed to this ride? Touching Farris, even as a necessity, was an assault on all the walls she had carefully built around her emotions. Being so close to him exposed all the lies she had told herself. That she was better off without him. That she no longer had feelings for him.

His hand brushed her thigh as he shifted in the saddle. "You okay back there?" he asked. The breeze had picked up.

"I'm fine."

Farris kicked his heels, and the horse took off. India leaned into Farris's back, her cheek resting at his spine. His body was a shield against the icy air.

Tears formed in her eyes and froze on her lashes. It was only the wind making her eyes water. She had shed too many tears five years ago over Farris Quinn. Never again.

Four

Farris was in hell. How else could he explain the fact that he could see and taste and touch heaven and yet not really hold on to it?

He wanted to ride for miles, far beyond the boundaries of his own property. The sensation of infinite peace—intermingled with driving lust—was both wonderful and torturous. As long as he kept moving, India would be his. With her body pressed against him, he felt invincible.

She was nervous around him. How could he blame her? In her wary gaze, he saw distrust—of his motives, his words, his intentions. It was surprising she had come to Aspenglow at all. Only the bond between India and his mother had wrought this miracle.

He was selfish enough to relish the result of his machinations, even if the enjoyment was temporary.

When they returned to the ranch, only a pink stain remained in the sky. He dismounted outside the barn and helped India down. When he put a hand to her cheek, he frowned. "You're freezing. I'm sorry about that."

In the dim light of dusk, he couldn't read her eyes. She took a step backward, breaking any connection, physical or otherwise. "I enjoyed the ride," she said. "Your ranch is lovely, Farris."

When she turned and headed for the house, he felt a jagged rip in the region of his heart. He was supposed to be so damn smart. Why, then, had he destroyed the single greatest investment he ever made?

India was cold through to the bone. Part of her discomfort was the result of too much time spent outside in the frigid Wyoming winter. Harder still to combat was the despair that shrouded her in hopelessness.

She hadn't gotten over Farris. She had been lying to herself for five years. Denial was a kind of self-preservation, but still.

How had she believed such a ridiculous fabrication? Today, with her body so close to his, the truth had been impossible to miss. She still wanted her ex-husband. But it was even more than physical. After all these years, she hadn't stopped loving him. Maybe. To acknowledge such a thing would be to admit that her life was ruined.

While Farris's amazing horse had been carrying them over the landscape, the minutes had almost felt like flying. Her life back in New York, the life she told herself was fulfilling and wonderful, seemed like an odd dream.

She was in so much trouble. Instead of worrying about Dottie, India should be worrying about *herself*. The trap was clear. If she stayed—and of course she must—she had to figure out a way to keep her distance from Farris.

Not physically—that was impossible. They were living under the same roof. But emotionally. No more cozy horseback rides. No in-depth conversations about the past. Nothing personal at all.

To put it another way, she and Farris were like a divorced couple sharing custody, in this case of a grown woman.

She left Farris to care for his horse and escaped into the house, going in search of Dottie. Farris's mother looked much better now that she had taken a good rest.

India paused in the open doorway. "Are you ready for dinner?"

Dottie ran a brush through her hair and stood. She'd been at the small vanity, fussing with her makeup. Her color was good, and her eyes were bright. "I'm starving," she said. "I usually like a snack midafternoon, but I slept right through."

"Something smells wonderful," India said.

On the way toward the dining room, Dottie linked her arm with India's. "How was the horseback ride?"

India stiffened unconsciously. "You knew about that?"

Dottie looked at her oddly. "Farris sent me a text, so I wouldn't worry."

"Of course," India said, feeling foolish. "It was a cold

ride, but interesting. He showed me all the improvements he's made since I was here last."

"He's worked hard," Dottie said. "Sometimes I think the boy never sleeps."

The *boy* joined them just as the housekeeper brought in bowls of hearty beef stew, along with homemade corn bread. On such a cold night, the comfort food was welcome. India didn't enjoy hers as much as she should have. She was too occupied with studying Farris out of the corner of her eye.

He barely looked at her, his attention focused instead on Dottie. As mother and son chatted, India ate in silence. Farris's demeanor was no different than usual. But when he finally glanced in her direction, his expression was closed off, much like those last months of their marriage.

She hated that expression on his face. She'd had nightmares about it, had cried over it. Why had Farris shut her out? Why had he gone from indulgent husband to haughty stranger in a matter of weeks? Five years ago, she had wanted to ask the question louder and louder still until the truth exploded from him. In the end, to preserve her sanity, she had convinced herself that the answer didn't matter, because he had clearly stopped loving her.

Now those same nausea-inducing questions burned in her gut. She had thought she was over him, damn it. She desperately *wanted* to be over him. Why, then, was she suddenly unsure of herself? And why did old, painful questions seem relevant again?

The evening didn't improve. Over dessert—warm apple pie with ice cream—the master of the house dropped a bombshell. "I'm flying to New York in the morning. I'll be up before dawn, so I won't see either of you before I go."

Though India was startled by the abrupt news, it was Dottie who quizzed him. "Why, son? You were just there ten days ago."

"And I have to go again." His irritation was clear, but India didn't think it was really directed at his mother.

India spoke up, determined not to let him ignore her. "How long will you be gone?" Her question was more than idle curiosity. With Dottie to be looked after, India needed to have any pertinent details.

It was odd that Farris hadn't mentioned the trip while he and India were out this afternoon. It seemed like the kind of information she should know.

He dipped a spoon into his dessert, not looking at either woman for a few moments. "It's only an overnight trip," he said. "I have to sign some papers, interview a new hire. And I'll check on Mom's apartment, too."

Dottie bounced in her chair. "Oh, good," she said. "Will you bring me a few things if I make a list?" She grinned at India. "When he went back week before last, he was in too much of a hurry. But I keep thinking of odds and ends I want." She switched her attention back to her son. "Maybe you could use one of my carry-ons in the closet."

Farris rolled his eyes, his smile wry as Dottie cajoled him. "Whatever you want, Mother dearest. Your wish is my command."

His silliness delighted Dottie. "You're such a good boy."

It was India's turn to jump into the game. "I doubt

many people describe Farris Quinn as a good boy. More of a dangerous shark, maybe."

The room fell silent. A tiny frown gathered between Dottie's brows. "With outsiders, maybe. Never with family."

"It was a joke," India said weakly, well aware that she had stepped over some invisible line.

Farris shrugged. "It's okay, Mother. India has seen me in business settings more than you have."

India swallowed the lump in her throat. "I'm sorry, Dottie. Farris is a fine man. You did a wonderful job raising him all on your own."

Apparently, Dottie was confused. "If he's such a *fine man*, why did you leave him?"

India shot Farris an incredulous look. She stood abruptly. "Excuse me." Her heart pounded with shock as she turned and fled.

"Mother, what were you thinking?" Farris groaned and pressed two fingers in the center of his forehead, where a knifelike pain stabbed.

Dottie wilted, her expression both worried and defiant. "Well, it's true. We're all living in this house together being so sophisticated and tolerant, but the truth is, that woman abandoned you. I love her dearly, but she disappointed me."

Farris was shocked. "I had no idea you felt that way. I'm sorry, Mother, sorry I didn't tell you the truth. I should have been more honest with you when it happened."

"Honest about what?"

Farris firmed his jaw, his stomach churning. "I ended

the marriage, not India. I did and said things that made it impossible for her to stay."

"Farris!" Dottie's horror was real.

"Things happen in a marriage, things that only the two people involved truly understand. It was a long time ago. I don't wish to discuss it."

His feisty mother gave him a narrow-eyed glare. "What about what *I* want? I don't appreciate being left out in the cold. What happened today on that horseback ride? Is that why you're leaving? You never said anything before about this New York trip."

Farris searched for the right words. Dottie had hit the nail on the head. Being with India today had scared him. He was flying out in the morning to avoid temptation.

"I told you why. I have papers to deal with, and my CFO wants me to sign off on a new employee. The decision has been made, I think. But my rubber stamp makes everyone feel better."

His only parent stared at him until his scalp tingled. Surely, lying to one's mother was a mortal sin.

Dottie wiped her mouth with the lovely cloth napkin and stood.

Automatically, Farris stood, as well.

She shook her head slowly. "This may not work out, son. If I have to go back to New York, so be it. I don't want to cause pain to either you *or* India."

"India and I are fine," he said. *Lie number two.* "We both want to help you take care of your health and for you to be happy."

"I'm plenty happy," Dottie said, heading for the door. "It's you I worry about."

His mother's parting shot echoed in Farris's head

throughout his sleepless night and all the way across the country the following day on a succession of planes.

When he landed in New York, the city was shrouded in gray mist and rain. Cold, but not cold enough for snow. Farris hunched into his coat collar and waved down the car he had ordered.

The limo was an indulgence. But it afforded him the opportunity for complete privacy as he made the mad dash into the city. He had the driver take him directly to Quinn headquarters. The aforementioned papers were soon signed, and Farris met the impressive woman who was to start Monday. Her résumé was stellar.

Truth be told, Farris was no longer needed at this empire he had built. Because he had surrounded himself with good people, the ship sailed on, even if Farris was in Wyoming. Some days he didn't know if that was a good thing or a bad thing.

By four, he was unlocking the door to his penthouse apartment on Park Avenue, just a few blocks away from Dottie's abode. He couldn't help remembering the first time he brought India here. They had been dating for three months at that point. Farris had cooked for her and watched, smiling, as India stood at the huge plate-glass windows and looked out over the city, her expression awed.

In the middle of dinner, she had asked him point-blank if he was rich. He'd tried to avoid answering, but of course she had already known as soon as she saw his home. Unfortunately for him, as far as he could tell, she wasn't overly impressed.

India had always preferred simple meals to gourmet experiences. Though she cherished the wedding ring he gave her, he'd had to lie about the cost of her engagement diamond. India loved the emerald-cut, two-carat stone, but if she had known how much it cost, she would never have worn it.

Now that he thought about it, perhaps he was more of a liar than he realized. Lying in order to make people comfortable was still lying.

He passed the bedroom where he normally slept and went to stand in the doorway of the master suite. After India left him, he hadn't been able to sleep alone in that huge king-size bed. If he closed his eyes, he could almost hear her laughter.

Painful memories mixed with fond ones. India was a cover hog. Fortunately, Farris was hot-natured. Many a night he had awakened to find that she had dragged the sheet and comforter to her side of the bed.

The past five years had not been easy. Now he had complicated his life even further by asking India to be Dottie's companion. Would he come to regret that decision?

Didn't he already regret it?

The silence in the apartment mocked him. He was alone.

The morning Farris left for New York City, Dottie didn't show up for breakfast. India wasn't too alarmed, but it did feel odd to eat solo in the dining room. After her solitary meal, she went to Dottie's door and listened.

India was pretty sure she heard a television running. Maybe Dottie had slept restlessly and was having a slow start. Because India wasn't sure of the parameters of this new relationship, she didn't knock. Instead, she went to the workout room for half an hour and then show-ered and changed.

By the time she was done, she decided it would be okay to check on her charge a little more aggressively. Fortunately, Dottie's door was open this time. India found her sitting on the bed, flipping through an enve-lope of photographs.

"Good morning," India said cheerfully.

Dottie looked up with a smile. "Hello, dear. Sorry I slept so late."

"No worries. Would you like me to bring you some breakfast?"

"Thanks, but not necessary. A few weeks ago, Farris ordered me a minifridge. It's plugged in over there in the corner. I know that sounds terribly decadent, but I kind of love it now. If I feel like being a hermit, I have everything I need right here."

That might be an exaggeration, but India could tell Dottie's pleasure was genuine. "It's a very cozy setup. I'm glad you're so comfortable." India paused, but then gave in to impulse. "May I ask you something?" she said.

Dottie cocked her head. "Of course."

"Why didn't you take the blue room for yourself?"

The older woman wrinkled her nose. "To be honest, I was trying to give my son some privacy. He and I were planning to stay here for a number of weeks, maybe months. I didn't want him to feel stifled."

"But now *I'm* there in the blue room," India said, feeling awkward and slightly embarrassed. "Is there another space I could use?"

"Not really." Dottie stood and paced, her expression

agitated. "I want to apologize for yesterday. I spoke to you harshly. Farris admitted the divorce was his fault. I'll say this and nothing more. You could give him another chance."

What was India supposed to say to that? Maybe truth was the only option. "I didn't want to end our marriage. But there were problems. And Farris was not interested in working things out."

"I find that hard to believe." Dottie put a hand to her mouth and sat down again.

"I don't want to speak ill of your son. Please know that."

"Understood. Please, India. Tell me what you want to say."

"I thought when I married Farris that I had the family I yearned for. And in the beginning, I did have. But he pulled away from me. He kept secrets. At one time, he was my best friend. My dearest lover. And then…" She trailed off, her throat tight. It was no fun to rehash the old hurts and failures.

"Then what?" Dottie's round-eyed expression echoed a combination of concern and bewilderment.

India shrugged, helpless to rewrite history. "Farris changed. I didn't ask a lot of questions, because I didn't want to cause conflict. But that was wrong of me. That's not how a marriage should be. I knew I deserved better."

Dottie wept, silent tears that made silvery marks on her flushed cheeks. "I am so sorry. I thought it was the other way around. I thought you found someone else."

"No." India's laugh held little amusement. "I *have* moved on, though, Dottie. I appreciate your concern, but these things are between Farris and me. I'm here because I love you."

Dottie dried her face with a cotton hankie. "He was over the moon when you accepted his marriage proposal. I had never seen him so happy."

"Well, it ended. What can I say? But I did try one last time to pry him out of his awful shell. I gave him an ultimatum. Either talk to me—tell me what was wrong—or I was walking out. Silly me, I thought that would be the jolt he needed to open up and finally let me know what he was thinking. How wrong could I be? He watched, stone-faced, as I packed a bag and left our home."

India sat down in an armchair, her legs suddenly like spaghetti. She had never told the whole story to anyone, not even her closest girlfriends. The rift in her marriage had been puzzling, agonizing and embarrassing. And when it was over, once again she was like that scared fifteen-year-old girl, orphaned and alone.

Dottie sighed deeply, wringing her hands. "Men," she said, the single word laden with disgust. "I love my boy dearly, but even I know that he can't be an easy person to deal with in an intimate relationship. I wish I could help. I wish I could explain."

"It's not up to you, Dottie. Whatever secrets he carries with him are buried deep." Too much time had passed, too much water swirling under the proverbial bridge.

Finally, Dottie rose to her feet. "I don't want us to mope all day. Why don't we go to the den and work on more pictures?"

"That's a great idea," India said, projecting enthusiasm, even though all she wanted to do was climb into bed and pull the covers over her head.

Over the next few hours, she and Dottie actually began to make a dent in the organizational nightmare that was the family photo stash. India worked backward from the present, while Dottie began putting the earlier years in order.

At one point, India cued up a playlist on her phone. The music filled the silences and made the minutes pass more quickly. By dinnertime, they had created something approaching a system.

Dottie still protested throwing away prints, but India was adamant. No one needed twenty-seven blurry photos of bison in Yellowstone. Tough love.

The housekeeper summoned them at six. Without the master of the house in residence, the meal was more informal. Dottie and India sat across from each other near the head of the table.

Dottie ate enthusiastically, perhaps because she had skipped lunch. "Wonderful," she said, digging into her chicken piccata.

India agreed. "It's a shame Farris is missing this."

"Don't you remember, dear? He's allergic to capers, mildly at least. They upset his stomach terribly."

India hid her confusion and disbelief. On their first wedding anniversary, India had made a big fuss. She told Farris she didn't want to go to a restaurant. What she proposed instead was that *she* cook for him. Over the course of their relationship, he had taken her to some of the finest eateries in the world. Now it was her turn to pamper her man.

She had served chicken piccata.

What the hell? Farris had eaten every bite and asked for seconds. Yet another thing he hadn't been honest about...

How could a husband who was so careful not to hurt his young wife's feelings become distant and aloof a mere two years later?

Dottie's inadvertent but stunning revelation occupied India's mind throughout the remainder of the meal and in the hours that followed. Though the two women watched a lighthearted romantic comedy on a streaming channel, India would be hard-pressed to describe the plot.

Why did she care if Farris was allergic to capers? Their relationship was dead. Period. Far past the point of CPR.

At last, Dottie noticed that India was frazzled. "Don't fret, India. Farris will be home tomorrow. Maybe then you can get some answers. Or maybe he might talk to me."

"No!" India was horrified. "No, Dottie. Swear to me you won't say a word about any of this. I need you to promise. I'm not kidding."

Her former mother-in-law nodded sadly. "Okay. You're right. It's not my place to interfere."

India swallowed hard. Of course she wanted answers, but to what end? Her marriage was over.

The fact that Farris was coming home tomorrow meant nothing to her. Nothing at all.

Five

Farris did *not* come home the next day. Or the next or the next. In fact, by the time the weekend rolled around, he had been away from Wyoming for six nights. The first couple of afternoons, he copied both Dottie and India on his texts that gave vague details about why he had gotten hung up in New York and why he wasn't returning yet.

But eventually, Dottie was the only one getting info. India refused to let her feelings be hurt. Farris had no obligation to communicate with his ex-wife.

Still, all the rationalizations in the world didn't appease the tight, achy knot in her chest. On Saturday at breakfast, she decided it was time for a change of scenery. "How are you feeling today?" she asked as they enjoyed Belgian waffles, raspberries and fresh-squeezed orange juice.

Dottie wiped a drip of syrup from her chin. "I feel great."

"What would you think about going for a drive? The sun is shining. It's above freezing today. We could even stop in town for lunch if you want to shake things up."

"I'd love that."

"What vehicles do we have?"

"Farris bought me a new Range Rover when he realized I was going to be living here. He wanted me to be able to drive around the ranch without worrying about getting stuck anywhere."

India raised an eyebrow. "Nice. Do you want to drive for our excursion, or shall I play chauffeur?"

Dottie waved a hand. "Oh, you drive, please. I don't really enjoy being behind the wheel."

While India was in her room changing clothes and gathering her things, she remembered suddenly that Farris had tried to buy her a similarly expensive vehicle when they first came to Wyoming as newlyweds. She had declined. In New York, she never drove at all, and when she and Farris were out West, she rarely went anywhere on her own. The expense had seemed not only extravagant, but unnecessary.

It took Dottie fifteen minutes to remember where the keys were, but finally they were on their way. The vehicle's interior was luxurious and still smelled like new leather. The heated seats kept them comfortable.

India steered a circuitous route west and then slightly north, intersecting the highway at Moose Junction and taking the southern turn. The Tetons were striking today, the sun gleaming off jagged snowcapped peaks. Even farther south in Teton Village, the skiers would be out in full force.

Dottie was quiet, but she had a smile on her face. India found herself nostalgic for the time when all of this had been novel to her. Farris had been as eager as a new puppy, determined that she would love Wyoming as much as he did.

In the town of Jackson, India found a parking space on the street near a restaurant both women liked. India helped her passenger out of the car and held her arm as they maneuvered the two steps to the porch that stretched around two sides of the building.

Over vegetarian lasagna and wonderful homemade bread, Dottie chattered away. India knew in an instant that this spontaneous get-out-of-the-house plan had succeeded. To go from the hustle and bustle of New York to relative isolation on the ranch in Jackson Hole must have been hard for Dottie, even though the move had been her choice.

India wanted to ask about Farris, but she held her tongue. It was better for her mental health not to know. She concentrated on her companion.

Over coffee and dessert, Dottie fixed India with a mischievous look. "I know you don't like talking about your marriage, so I'll start further back. I remember that you're an only child…and that you lost your parents when you were fifteen. That must have been terribly hard."

India nodded, stirring cream into her cup, watching the dark brown change to pale mocha. "I've lived almost half my life without them now. Sometimes it's hard to remember their faces. But yes, it was devastating."

"Will you tell me what happened? Farris never said much about the details. I assumed he was protecting your privacy."

"My parents were arguing. They did that a lot, actually. One of those oil-and-water couples who thrived on high drama and confrontation. For a kid like me, it was unsettling. But at least I knew they loved each other."

"I've met people like that."

"Then you understand. Anyway, I came home from school and caught them in the middle of a huge blowup. My father was a gambler, everything from poker to lottery tickets. Occasionally he would go to a Gamblers Anonymous meeting, but mostly he would convince my mother that he had his impulses under control."

"And did he?"

"No. Not ever, really. I think he just became good at hiding things." *Like Farris, actually.* "But on this particular occasion, my mother found out that he had bet a huge sum on a horse race. The bet was a bad one. He used our house as collateral. We were going to lose everything."

"Oh, sweetie. How awful."

"The shouting got worse. Eventually, my mother came to my door to tell me she and Daddy were going for a drive. I think that was her way of saying they didn't want to have an ugly confrontation in front of me. Anyway, they were clearly upset and angry when they left. Less than half an hour later, my father ran a red light. I've always assumed he was distracted by their fight.

Their car was broadsided by a tractor-trailer truck. They were both pronounced dead at the scene."

Dottie paled. "India. I had no idea."

"I lived in foster care until I turned eighteen. There was a small insurance stipend, enough for me to get a studio apartment in a wretched neighborhood. I was afraid Farris would think I wanted him for his money, but that was the farthest thing from my mind. What I really wanted was to *belong* to someone again. I thought I had found that, but I was wrong."

Though Dottie professed herself thrilled with the outing, the unusual activity had clearly tired her. She napped for several hours in the afternoon.

India was filled with nervous energy. Three times, she almost texted Farris. The communication could be light and easy. A brief note to tell him how his mother had spent the morning. But on every occasion, India chickened out.

Finally, in desperation, she forced herself to do five punishing miles on the treadmill. When she was exhausted and dripping with sweat, she showered and changed. Then she made her way to the great room and riffled through some of the photos she and Dottie hadn't sorted yet.

The ones of Farris were impossible to ignore. She could almost *see* the development of his personality over the years. The adolescent Farris was already driven to succeed, presumably by the fact that his father had abandoned him. Perhaps Farris had wanted the bigamist to see that a smart, focused boy didn't need a second-hand father, one who belonged to someone else.

Because India was alone, and the house was quiet, her thoughts landed on the one problem she hadn't quite figured out how to handle. She was still physically attracted to her husband. But he wasn't her husband.

She had been with only one man since her divorce, a colleague at another station. The sex was good, but ultimately unsatisfying in an emotional sense. She had known, even lying in his bed, that this new man in her life was never going to be her great passion.

Because honesty had become a touchstone for her, she told him the truth. They had sex a few more times, but eventually things fizzled.

The trouble was, a woman her age needed sex, wanted sex. But since she wasn't interested in bar hookups or one-night stands, she found herself obstinately alone. She didn't mind her own company. And she was never bored. But there were many nights when she ached for a warm male in her bed, for strong arms to hold her— for the chance to start over again and build a life that would include marriage and children.

If she really was such a fan of the truth, it was time to admit the unthinkable. She *had* come here for Dottie *and* to spend time with her ex-husband again. She was never going to be happy in love if she compared every man she met to Farris. He had ruined her, setting the bar high.

What if she tried having sex with Farris while she was here? Either she would find out that she needed to fight harder for the family she wanted with him, or she would discover that her ex-husband still clung stubbornly to his secrets.

Was the tiniest chance of success worth the terrible risk of failure?

She had never found closure five years ago. Perhaps that was why she was still searching for an elusive dream. She hadn't found Mr. Right in New York, because Mr. Wrong in Wyoming irrevocably claimed her.

Her skin hummed with arousal. Her heartbeat fluttered. With Dottie sleeping, India did the one thing she knew she should not do. She walked down the hall, passed her own room and entered the master suite. It seemed prudent to close the door behind her, so there would be no surprises.

As she stood there, scanning the spot where she had felt most content, her heart sank in confusion and shock. Nothing was the same.

Not paint colors, not bedclothes, not even the arrangement of the furniture. It was as if Farris had intentionally wiped away every trace of his marriage.

Apparently, he had wanted to start over, completely from scratch.

Well, he'd succeeded, she thought bleakly. Her stomach was in a knot. Being erased from a person's life was not a pleasant sensation. Of course, if she hadn't trespassed, she would be none the wiser.

Now that she was in the tiger's lair, she snooped unashamedly. The book on the nightstand was a hardback new release from a true-crime writer Farris enjoyed. A glass of water, half-empty, sat there, too. She picked it up and took a sip of the tepid liquid, imagining her lips touching the rim where his had been.

Moments later when India flung open the closet, Farris's scent washed over her. Masculine, evocative, notes of lime and evergreen. As familiar to her as her own bodywash or perfume. She touched a shirt, a dinner jacket. It was surprising to see dress clothes here. In her experience, Farris lived very casually in Wyoming.

After the closet, the bathroom was next. This, thank goodness, was more familiar. Short of a complete remodel, it would be impossible to change. The luxurious shower enclosure was the same. Even the navy waffle-weave robe hanging on a hook was one she remembered.

When a text dinged on her phone, she jumped guiltily. It was only a reminder about a dental appointment... one she would need to cancel. Still, the interruption was enough to jolt her out of her trip down memory lane.

She flushed, though there was no one to see her.

Curiosity had compelled her to invade Farris's privacy. Now she wished she hadn't. Her discoveries upset her.

For the remainder of the day, she moped and brooded... subtly, of course. There was Dottie to entertain. The older woman woke up from her nap with a burst of energy. She and India worked on the photos. A huge box was delivered just before dark. It contained the albums Dottie had ordered.

"Let's start the first one," she said gleefully.

India had to put on the brakes. "It's almost time to eat, and besides, we really shouldn't begin until we have all the pictures sorted. Otherwise, we'll end up going back and ripping things out to start all over again."

Dottie pouted. "You sound just like Farris. Always raining on my parade."

India grinned. "I'm sorry. But you know I'm right."

After dinner, the two of them played Scrabble for an hour. That was about all Dottie could handle. Her lack of stamina worried India. Her former mother-in-law had changed dramatically in only five years. Farris insisted that Dottie had made peace with her diagnosis, but what about him? He was very protective of the mother who had raised him mostly on her own. How would Farris react when the only parent he cared about was gone? He would be all alone in the world.

Once Dottie was tucked in, India knew she had to do something or go stir-crazy. After bundling up in all her layers, plus mittens and a heavy scarf, she sneaked outside, making sure to reset the alarm and take a key. With the housekeeper gone for the evening, Dottie was alone inside.

Out under the winter moon—a wolf moon, if she recalled—India inhaled the unmistakable scent of winter, filling her lungs with air that was clean and pure. She stayed close to the house, mindful of coyotes.

The stars overhead sparkled in a stunning array. Even the Milky Way was visible. After being back in New York for so long, she had almost forgotten what the sky looked like in a really dark place.

As beautiful as the night was, loneliness struck hard, reminding her that Aspenglow was no longer her home. She kept walking, refusing to give in to the dark thoughts dogging her heels. This time with Dottie was precious and temporary. At some point, India would return to New York, and her life would get back to normal.

She was lucky to have a wide circle of friends and an active social calendar. She loved her job and the challenges it offered. She had healed emotionally. There was no reason in the world for her to be melancholy.

But the feeling persisted, robbing the night of its joy. She wanted Farris's arms around her, yearned to bask in the warmth of his big, muscular body. Was that urge nothing more than sexual attraction?

What would happen if she acted on those impulses?

Eventually, cold toes and fingers forced her back inside. Under the stinging spray of a hot shower, she gave herself a pep talk. It wasn't like her to wallow in self-pity. From now on, Farris Quinn was just another guy.

It was a whopper of a lie, but she was trying to think positively.

It felt good to curl up in a comfy bed with an interesting book. She read for an hour and then yawned so many times in a row she knew it was time to turn out the light. Sleep came almost instantly.

Sometime around three a.m., a noise awakened her. Not very loud, but close by. Her heart racing, she sat straight up in bed.

It wouldn't be Dottie. Farris's mother took medication to help her sleep and thus slumbered deeply.

Maybe the sound was outside.

She listened intently, almost forgetting to breathe. There it was again. Footsteps? An intruder? Had she forgotten to set the alarm when she came inside?

Another sound had her climbing out of bed and grabbing the nearest weapon. The gas-log fireplace was flanked on the hearth by a set of useless though decorative tools. One of them was about to get used, decorative or not.

India grabbed the brass poker and tiptoed toward

the door. She didn't want to open the door at all. But if she called 911, help would be slow in coming, given the ranch's remote location.

Adrenaline shored up her courage. Stealthily, she hefted the poker, turned the knob and opened the door. Every cell in her body jumped to high alert.

Earlier, she had turned off the hall light before going to bed. In the interim, someone had flipped the switch again, now illuminating the small foyer that connected the two bedrooms. A large man stood there, juggling two pieces of luggage.

"Oh," she said, feeling foolish. "It's you." Heat flooded her body. She had thought about him for hours, and now here he was.

In an effort to ignore the disturbing fact that she was so desperately glad to see him, she went on the offensive. "I had no idea you were coming home tonight. You scared the hell out of me."

Farris looked tired but no less sexy. There were shadows beneath those beautiful blue eyes. His black hair was mussed. The ends of a navy silk tie hung from his jacket pocket. His once-crisp dress shirt was open at the collar. "I told Mother," he said. "I sent her a text around eight tonight."

"Dottie went to bed early. I suppose she forgot to mention it to me…or assumed it didn't matter."

He set down his bags and reached for her. India was shocked for a split second. But then she realized he meant to disarm her. She'd still been holding the poker over her head. Farris tugged it from her grasp and leaned it in the corner, his expression quizzical. "Were you really prepared to bash in someone's skull?

The India I remember didn't even like to use mouse-traps in the barn."

"People change," she said. Now that the immediate *intruder* emergency was over, she found herself weak and shaky. Not to mention feeling at a distinct disadvantage. Her long-sleeved flannel pajamas were neither new nor particularly flattering. She had packed them knowing they would be good for the cold Wyoming winter nights.

She certainly hadn't expected to encounter her ex-husband while wearing the dismally unsexy pj's.

"I'm sorry I scared you," he said quietly.

His body language said he was not in the mood for a fight, verbal or otherwise. India could relate. She wrapped her arms around herself, glancing down to see if her nipples were poking against her top.

Turned out, they were. But there was nothing she could do about it, so maybe Farris wouldn't notice.

India sighed. "It's okay," she muttered. "I let my imagination run away with me. I should have known it was you. Why so late, though? I thought the last flight came in around nine thirty."

"I missed my connection in Salt Lake. They were going to put me up in a hotel and get me on the six a.m. flight tomorrow morning. I decided I'd rather rent a car."

"You drove three hundred miles in the dark through the mountains?"

He shrugged, giving her a small grin that still had enough wattage to make her legs tremble. "At least half of it was interstate."

She shook her head in disgust. "Men," she said.

"What can I say? I wanted to get home."

"If you were in such a big hurry to get home, why did you extend your trip?"

Farris's sculpted jaw jutted. His eyes flashed blue heat. "I think you know the answer to that, India."

Six

Farris watched as India's cheeks and throat flushed and then lost color entirely. Her hazel eyes widened, filled with a wary expression that frustrated him.

She chewed her bottom lip. "I don't know what you mean."

"Are we playing it that way?" he asked pleasantly. He studied her as she practically stuttered. Was he actually getting turned on by those god-awful navy pajamas with the pink poodles? Maybe so. The truth was, it didn't matter what she wore. He wanted her. He would always want her.

When she didn't say a word, he cocked his head and stared at her. "I like your hair," he said. The silky blond locks brushed her jaw.

India shook her head slowly. "No, you don't. You always talked about how much you liked it long."

Interesting. "But now that you've cut it, I see how well it frames your face. The style suits you. Besides, what *I* want doesn't matter anymore, does it?"

"I should go to bed," she said, the words barely a whisper.

"You asked me why I stayed away so long."

"I don't really care," she said, paling further, her expression hunted.

"I think you do, Inkie. I think you're battling the same thing I am."

"And that would be?"

She was trying so hard to be nonchalant and sassy, but he saw through her bravado. "Temptation," he said. "I stayed in New York almost a whole damn week, because I don't trust myself to live under the same roof with you."

India swayed, her gaze locked on his. "That's not true."

He reached out and ran a fingertip down her smooth cheek. Her skin was warm and soft. Already he could imagine what she would look like when he stripped her out of those dreadful pajamas.

"It *is* true. And at the risk of sounding arrogant, I think you feel it, too. Tell me you don't, and I'll never mention it again. Tell me you aren't tempted."

His sweet adversary huffed a frantic little breath. "Why are you doing this?"

"You're going to be here for several months. We should clear the air. Lay our cards on the table. Be straight with each other."

India stared at him. Her gaze was darker now, her face flushed again. "That's a terrible string of clichés."

"What can I say? You throw me off my game. Always have."

It was a bad idea to be having this conversation right now. The middle of the night was the witching hour. Defenses were down. Sleep beckoned. People made bad decisions in moments like these.

"You're intimating that you want me?" she said, her body language either wary or braced or both. "You resisted me well enough before."

"I'm not *intimating* anything. I'm saying it flat out. I want you."

She shifted, moving forward just enough to place her hand, palm flat, over his breastbone. "We're not husband and wife anymore. We're not married."

His heart pounded. Her touch short-circuited his brain. "What does that have to do with sex and pleasure?" he muttered. "It's two entirely different things. Psychologists say that divorced people hook up all the time."

Her eyes were almost all pupil now. "Not when it's been five years." She put distance between them again, leaving him bereft.

"Fine. It was probably a bad idea anyway."

When he bent down, intending to pick up his carry-on, he almost lost his balance, because India launched herself at him. "Yes," she said. "Yes, I want you."

From her tone, he didn't think she was happy about it. But when her arms went around his neck, and she reached up on tiptoe to kiss him, he sucked in a breath and clutched her tightly. Shoulder to shoulder, hip to hip. Slamming his lips on hers with an intensity that bordered on desperation.

She felt the same and yet different. Still supple and soft in all the right places. But she had lost weight. He ran his hands from her narrow waist to her luscious ass, lifting her against him.

Gradually, the furor subsided and something else took its place, something seductive and unwise. That odd feeling was tenderness.

He couldn't afford that. This would only work if he concentrated on the physical. He would give her pleasure. Good sex. Great sex, if they were lucky. Nothing else. He sure as hell couldn't dwell on the past.

Without overthinking it, he scooped her into his arms, opened the door to his bedroom and carried her inside. Instead of using the overhead light, he flicked on a small lamp by the bed.

He waited for her to say something about the new furnishings, but she didn't. Instead, she stared up at him with an expression that was impossible to discern.

When he flipped back the covers and lowered her gently to the mattress, he saw her breasts move as she inhaled sharply. "You can change your mind," he said, cursing the sense of honor that forced out the words.

"No." She rose up on her elbows. "I want this. I want you."

Something about the words chipped at a raw wound in his heart. Danger hovered in the air, drawing both of them toward a place where there would be no turning back.

"I should take a shower," he said, suddenly remembering he was travel worn. "I'll be quick."

India shook her head. "No. If you do that, one of us will change our minds."

Ah. So even his prospective lover saw the pitfalls. "If that's true, doesn't it mean we're making a huge mistake?" He didn't know why he was pointing out the obvious.

"And if we are?"

The mocking challenge in her voice pushed him over the edge. "Fine," he said, the word like glass in his tight throat. "Give me three minutes. Not a shower. Just freshening up."

He took care of the necessary ablutions in one hundred and fifty seconds and exited the bathroom in a rush, expecting to find her gone.

But he was wrong. India had moved to the center of his bed. She was still on her back—one leg propped up. A few buttons of her pajama top were open, and she was caressing her own breast.

His heart thumped so hard against his ribs he thought he might be having a heart attack. While in the bathroom, he had undressed entirely and used a washcloth for the quickest rubdown on record. He had also put on his robe.

Now he was glad to have help disguising the fact that he was rock-hard. If she knew how very close he was to exploding with lust, he might frighten her away.

Slowly, he approached the bed. India barely seemed to notice. Her eyes were closed. A tiny smile tilted the corners of her mouth.

"India…" He said her name softly, not wanting to startle her.

When her eyelids fluttered and opened, her gaze was

hazy and warm. "There you are," she said, the words low and slurred.

He stopped beside the bed. "You should know something," he said gruffly. "I'm clean. I haven't been with a woman since you."

India sat straight up in bed, her eyes flashing with temper. "Don't do that. Don't lie to me. I trust you to protect your health, but don't spin me a tale. It's not necessary, and I don't want to hear it."

It had never occurred to him that she wouldn't believe the truth. He didn't know what to say.

Inkie had plenty of words for both of them. "If we're exchanging notes," she said, "I've only had one sexual relationship. He was a colleague. It ended over two years ago. We were always careful. That's it."

Pain seared the center of Farris's chest like a sword dipped in poison. He should *not* have been surprised. At all. India had been single for five years. Because of him.

He took several shallow breaths, trying to survive the unexpected blow that left him hollow. *Knowing* hurt far worse than simply suspecting. The news also deflated his erection. "Well, then," he said, "I suppose that's that."

While India watched, he shrugged out of his robe and tossed it on a nearby chair. He slid into bed beside her, tugging her arm until she lay down again. He pulled her close, feeling dizzy with disbelief. Five years. Five years since he had held her like this.

Meanwhile, India was so still and quiet he wasn't sure she was breathing.

Finally, she whispered something that caught at his

emotions and brought out his protective instincts. "I don't want to get hurt again," she said quietly. "You're not my husband. We aren't even friends. We're just two lonely adults looking for comfort."

Who was she trying to convince?

He swallowed hard. "I agree." The lie caught in his throat, but he told himself it was necessary. If India knew the truth about him—any of it—she would run far and fast.

She put a hand on his chest, not moving. Simply touching. "I was hoping you would be old and fat," she said.

After a shocked second, he burst out laughing. "Sorry to disappoint you."

"I'm not disappointed. Not exactly. In fact, right now, I'm glad to see that you're still a stud."

"I appreciate the compliment." He smiled against her hair, inhaling her scent…remembering.

"But, Farris…" She paused.

"Yes?"

"When you took off your robe, you weren't, um…"

"Hard?"

She nodded.

He exhaled, searching for the right answer. The diplomatic response. He couldn't tell her that the thought of his ex-wife in bed with another man destroyed him. "I've been awake for almost twenty-four hours. It's no reflection on you, Inkie. Trust me, I'll be good to go when it's time."

Without warning, she took him in her hand, squeezing carefully. "I'm pretty sure it's time, Mr. Quinn."

The gentle teasing left him floundering. How had he

ever thought they could have an impersonal fuck? This was the woman he had given his heart to…pledged his life to… Just because things were different now didn't mean he could treat her callously.

As she stroked him, his erection flexed and thickened. Quite painfully, in fact. He groaned when India used her fingernails on his balls. A shudder racked him from his scalp to his toes as white-hot pleasure flamed at every spot she touched.

"Wait," he gasped. "Slow down."

But apparently India was not in a mood to take orders, at least not from him. Before he could help her, she had stripped out of her pajama top and shimmied the bottoms down her shapely legs. Her panties sailed through the air.

"We'll need a condom," she said, the words entirely without inflection.

He rolled to his side and jerked open a drawer. Did latex go out of date? "These may not be any good," he said.

India froze for a moment. A tiny frown creased the area between her brows. "I'm on the pill," she said, the words flat. "The condom is only a backup."

Farris ripped open the package and dealt with the protection. Having India watch him made the act more intimate, more arousing. When he was ready, he rolled on his side to face her. She had assumed the same position.

Someone should paint her like this, he thought hazily as his brain turned to mush. The feminine curve from her hip to the valley at her narrow waist was poetry. Her pale-skinned breasts with raspberry tips beckoned him. He put a hand on her thigh. "I don't want to rush this," he said.

India took his hand and placed his palm over the place where her heart raced. "I'm not sure slow is an option."

He felt the thuds of her beating life force, wondering if she was half as excited as he was. Had he known when he invited her to come to Wyoming that this would happen? Had India herself had any inkling?

Humans were remarkably good at self-deception.

"Are you sure this is what you want?" He watched her face, seeking any sign of uncertainty. He had plenty of faults, but he wouldn't coerce her.

India's sudden smile was as surprising as it was sweet. Her hazel eyes with the intriguing mix of colors were clear. "Quit worrying, Farris. Your conscience can rest. We're using each other for mutual satisfaction. No harm, no foul."

She eased onto her back, her mocking expression urging him on. Hell, he didn't need a signed consent form. India wanted him. And she wasn't bothering to hide it.

Before he entered her, he slid two fingers between her legs, tested her soft warmth. Her sex was slick and hot. When he touched her most sensitive spot, her keening cry nearly made *him* come.

It was clear she was ready.

Slowly, he moved over her and settled between her thighs, feeling a rush of emotion that clogged his throat. *Danger. Danger.* Her eyelids fluttered shut. He didn't like that. Was she fantasizing about someone else?

He positioned the head of his erection and pushed

slowly. The feeling of being encased in a snug caress made his vision go black. Everything in him centered on his aching sex. But he wasn't so far gone that he forgot to give her the agreed-upon pleasure.

Balancing on one elbow, panting, he used his free hand to stroke her nipples gently, to tug. Watching the play of emotion on her face was a revelation.

Her pleasure stoked his higher, a hundred times. Maybe a thousand. When her legs wrapped around his waist, he went deeper. She linked her ankles at the small of his back, her heels digging into his spine.

Somehow, he had forgotten how good it was. The two of them. Naked skin to naked skin. Maybe the sexual amnesia was a form of self-protection. Now that the blinders were off, how would he ever give this up again? When they were married, he had left her bed… had given her up for reasons that he thought were good ones at the time. Was it wrong to take her now when he had hurt her so badly before?

With India arching her back and forcing him a final centimeter, his last ounce of control snapped and vanished in a cloud of need. He surged hard, all the way in.

She cried out his name. Every hair on his body stood. He trembled as if he had a fever. And maybe he did. Maybe it was fatal.

When India returned home, Farris's world would go dark again.

He ignored his painful thoughts, choosing to concentrate on the carnal instead. He set up a rhythm that tormented them both.

India hadn't said a word since she uttered his name. Her eyes were still closed, shutting him out.

He was pissed suddenly. Angry. "Look at me, India."

The snap in his voice got through to her. She obeyed, her gaze locking on his.

He ground the base of his sex against her sensitive spot. "Come for me, Inkie. Come."

She gasped and moaned. He felt the shudder that racked her body as her orgasm crested, peaked, slid down the other side. Only then did he let himself go all the way, his vision dark, punctuated only with pulses of light that synced to his heartbeat.

Time passed. Who knew how long? It seemed prudent to stand up and deal with the condom, but he couldn't feel his legs. He expected India to push at his shoulder any moment and demand to be released, but she was oddly quiet. Now that the deed was done, he suspected neither of them had words for this situation. He let himself drift, his face buried in her hair.

In that moment of blissful euphoria, he pondered telling her the truth. He didn't expect a reunion, even if she forgave him. Some sins were beyond redemption. Of all the mistakes he had ever made, cutting himself off from India had been the worst.

And the secrets…so many secrets…

At last, she stirred. "Let me up," she said.

He rolled to one side and watched as she slid off the bed, grabbed her pajamas and went to the bathroom.

When she returned, there was no sign of the soft, warm woman who had made love to him so beautifully.

Her face was blank, wiped of all expression. She ran a hand through her hair, yawning. "Dottie will be up in a few hours. I need to get some sleep."

When she turned to walk out of the room, he panicked. "Wait," he said urgently. "Shouldn't we talk about this? Set some ground rules?" *Is this a one-and-done, or are you and I going to have sex again?*

India turned slowly, facing him. She shoved her hands in the pockets of her sleep pants. Her expression was wry, though not unkind. "Shall I quote you to yourself, Farris? *Not all the world's problems can be solved with a conversation.*"

He winced. India was not the same woman he had known. She was tougher, stronger, more willing to call him on his crap. "So what are you saying?"

She yawned again and tucked her hair behind her ears. "I don't have the emotional bandwidth to handle this *or* you right now. It's the middle of the night. Go to sleep, Farris. I'll see you at breakfast."

Inside her own room, India closed the door, locked it and leaned against it, mostly because she wasn't sure her knees would support her any longer.

What had she done?

She'd pretended to Farris that she was tired. Nothing could be further from the truth. Her body felt fizzy, and her skin was hot, even though the air was cool. How could she be both exhilarated and terrified at the same time?

One question had been answered tonight. Farris *wanted* her sexually. That was more than she had known before. She honestly had believed his lust for her burned out five years ago. Judging by their encounter tonight, that was a lie.

But if he was still attracted to her, why had he ended their marriage?

When she thought she could walk, she found her bed and burrowed beneath the covers, shaking uncontrollably. She needed sleep. But how could she sleep after what had just happened?

Images tumbled through her brain. The way he looked at her. The way he touched her. The desperation in his unguarded gaze.

For a man who was remarkably buttoned-up, he had let India see at least part of his true self tonight. She suspected both of them had tried to make the moment physical only. She certainly wanted it to be that way. But once they were in bed together, all the walls she had put in place to protect herself had crumbled.

She had stroked his hair, giddy with the ability to do so. His warm body had tangled with hers as if they were two puzzle pieces long since lost but finally reunited. Once, she had slipped. She'd said his name. With longing. With tenderness.

Almost immediately, she had locked down those impulses. Women could have impersonal sex. It was possible. But perhaps not with an ex-husband one still cared about deeply. She hadn't known *how* deeply until tonight.

The sex might have been just sex for him, but for her it had uncovered a trove of lies—all the half-truths and rationalizations she had used to get herself through the last five years. Now she felt raw, vulnerable. Was she strong enough to play a dangerous game of pretend with the man who had broken her once before?

What was she hoping to gain? Did she even understand her own motives?

Finally, the trembling stopped. Her pulse slowed. Drowsiness claimed her. She had no answers. Even if she went home tomorrow, she would always have tonight.

Seven

The morning after Farris returned from New York, India lost her courage. Instead of going straight to breakfast, she made a detour to Dottie's room. The older woman was just exiting with a definite bounce in her step.

"Farris is home," Dottie exclaimed. "Did you hear him come in during the wee hours? I hope he didn't disturb you."

India managed not to blush, though she felt as if her wild night was written on her face. "I'm a pretty heavy sleeper. Didn't hear a thing."

Fortunately, Dottie chattered all the way down the hall and into the dining room. When Dottie saw Farris, she flung her arms around her son as if he had been away at war and not out of town for a business trip.

"I've missed you," she said, hugging him tightly.

Farris hugged his mother in return. Over Dottie's head, the other two adults exchanged a glance. India gave him a bland smile. Farris seared her with his sapphire laser eyes. She had to catch her breath and break the connection, or she would have dissolved in a puddle.

When they were finally seated, and the housekeeper brought in quiche lorraine and fresh grapefruit, Dottie kept the meal from being uncomfortable. She asked Farris a million questions about his trip.

"Did you go to my apartment?" she asked. "Did you bring my bag? Was everything okay?"

He wiped his mouth with a napkin. "I did, and I did, and everything was fine."

Dottie beamed. "Oh, good." She turned to India. "I have a woman who comes in twice a week to water my plants."

India raised an eyebrow. "That's a lot of plant watering. Couldn't you have bought more plants whenever you go back to New York?"

"Oh, no." Dottie shook her head firmly. "I've had a few of those flowers and herbs as long as I've had Farris."

"Mother is right," he said. "We've moved those pots a dozen times or more. I always knew we were home when she decided where the plants would go."

"That's sweet." India mulled that story over as they ate. Sometimes she forgot that Dottie and Farris had been so traumatized in the earlier years. For all her frail appearance now, Dottie Quinn was a strong woman. She had picked herself up and cared for her young son with no support at all. Yet she never spoke bitterly, at least not in India's hearing.

Farris didn't speak of his father at all, but clearly, he had been deeply affected by what had happened when he was a child. Those scars had been internalized. He had driven himself to be perfect. Successful. Impervious to rejection.

Dottie continued to carry the conversation. "India's boxes came," she told Farris. "Three huge ones."

"Boxes?" Farris directed the question to India.

"When I first flew out here to Wyoming, I didn't know how long I would be staying, so I only brought the basics. Once I realized that I would be with Dottie for several months, I asked a friend of mine to go to my apartment and pack up the rest of my winter clothes. I'll owe her one for this."

Dottie finished her meal and gave both of her companions a smile. "I have an idea. Farris, will you help India and me with the photo albums for an hour or two? You won't believe how much fun it is."

He reached out and patted her hand. "I'd love to, but I've been gone a week, and ranch chores are piling up."

Dottie's face fell. "I understand."

India hated to see the disappointment on the older woman's face. "Dottie," she said, "why don't we meet in the great room in half an hour? I need to speak to Farris privately for a few minutes."

Dottie stood, her uncertain gaze going from India to Farris and back. "Of course, my dear."

When India and Farris were alone in the room, India lowered her voice. "Don't you think you should be spending more time with your mother? If my being in the room makes it uncomfortable for you, I can invent a reason not to help today."

As she spoke, Farris's jaw jutted, and his eyes flashed. "I don't need you to lecture me on my responsibilities to my mother," he said tersely. "Dottie understands my workload. Besides, that's why I have you…so she won't feel lonely."

"I'm not a substitute for her dearest child."

He rounded the table and stopped when they were toe to toe. He had a good five inches on her, so she was forced to tilt her head back to give him the evil eye.

He lowered his voice, the words barely audible. "Do you really want to argue about *this*, or is there something else on your mind?"

She sucked in a breath. "No. Nothing."

Farris tucked a strand of hair behind her ear, his thumb lingering to caress her cheek. His beautiful masculine lips tilted in a soft smile. The light in his eyes warmed her. "Last night was amazing, India."

"Um…" What was she supposed to say? Clearly, she should have thought about a possible script for this awkward morning after. "It was nice."

Farris chuckled. "Your pretty rosy lips are pursed so tightly it looks like you sucked a lemon."

"I can't do this, Farris."

His smile faded. "Do what?"

"You know what," she said, barely whispering for fear the housekeeper would appear around the corner. "You. Me."

He took a step backward, immediately making her feel bereft.

Her throat was tight. She had no idea what to say

or do. "We need to think this through, Farris. Before things go any further. Too many people could get hurt. Me. Dottie."

His jaw jutted. The blue eyes were glacial now. "You don't think *I'm* in any danger of getting hurt?"

Suddenly, all the trauma and shock of their divorce washed over her in a deluge of regret and remembered pain. "I have no idea, Farris. I don't know you at all anymore. Maybe I never did. But I do know this. If I'm going to care for your mother, I sure as heck shouldn't sleep with her son."

He shook his head slowly. "The old India wasn't so uptight about sex. She *loved* sex, as I recall. Remember that time we did it in Central Park? At midnight? You couldn't stop laughing until I made you come."

"Don't do that." It had been the most magical night. A full moon. Spring breezes. And her new husband's hands on her body.

"Is it so easy for you?" he asked soberly, his gaze watchful. "Do you just shove everything behind a locked door and forget about it?"

Now she was angry. "I wouldn't have to forget about it if my *husband* hadn't ghosted me."

He frowned. "When did I ghost you?"

"Oh, come on, Farris. You were suddenly traveling all over the country. And when you *were* home, you barely looked at me. I couldn't understand what I had done wrong. But I suppose you were simply bored."

"Don't be absurd." He was pale now, his lips closed in a grim line.

"Do you want to give me another explanation?"

The air vibrated around them. Seconds passed. Ten.

Twenty. Finally, Farris dropped his head and sighed. "No. I don't. What's done is done."

Her heart shriveled. For a moment, she'd thought he might finally come clean with her. That he might tell her the truth. She swallowed hard. *What's done is done.* "That's true. So why complicate things with sex?"

Now his head shot up, and his gaze trapped hers. "Because we're both lonely. And sex is something we do really well."

The ache in her chest spread, along with confusion. "Why don't you have someone in your life, Farris?"

His expression was bleak. "I'm not very good with relationships. You might have noticed that."

"Maybe not with me. But that doesn't mean there isn't somebody else out there who could give you what you need."

"No such person exists. If it wasn't you, it wasn't anybody."

"You're not making sense."

"I have to get to work. The guys are waiting on me." He took two steps toward the door, stopped and came back to where she stood by the table. He kissed her lips softly, a butterfly caress. When he straightened, his gaze was inscrutable. "For the record, I want to be intimate with you while you're here. The ball is in your court. If you're willing for us to be together under those circumstances, let me know."

And then he walked out…

India was in no mood to sort photos. Hopefully, Dottie didn't notice her lack of enthusiasm. After two hours,

India reached her limit. "I need to get some fresh air, Dottie. What if we take our lunch outside somewhere?"

"It's too cold."

"We could eat in the car. Please. The change of scenery would do us both good."

Dottie searched her face. "Are you all right, India?"

"It's not easy being here with Farris." This seemed like a moment when the truth might be the best course.

Dottie winced. "I understand. And yes, of course. I'd love to have lunch with you. I have a favorite spot, actually. Down by the river. A glorious view of the Tetons."

India realized Dottie was talking about the same place where Farris and India had ended up on their horseback ride. How could she forget? "Let's do it," India said, smiling. "It will be fun."

While Dottie changed clothes, India spoke with the housekeeper and arranged for a picnic basket. It wasn't difficult. The noon meal was usually some kind of finger food, and since Farris rarely came back to the house midday, the impromptu jaunt would easily accommodate lunch.

In less than thirty minutes, they were on their way in the Range Rover. Dottie remembered to point out the turn where they had to leave the road and head toward the river. In no time at all, they spotted the water. India parked beside the picnic table where she and Farris had sat.

Trying to set out all the containers of food in the confines of the car was tricky. But the meal more than made up for any inconvenience. The two women ate mostly in companionable silence. The view spoke volumes.

The temperature was still mild for January. Eventually, the force of the sun beaming through the windshield heated up the interior of the vehicle to the point that Dottie was fanning herself.

"Open your door a crack. I will, too," India said. "We'll get some cross ventilation for a few minutes. And if you get cold, tell me."

Soon, the crisp breeze made their nest far more comfortable. India finished her roast beef sandwich on sourdough and rummaged in a basket for a chocolate chip cookie. The thermos of lemonade was delicious.

Dottie ate more slowly. She sighed, leaning back in her seat. "This is lovely. What a good idea you had."

India glanced at her passenger, intending to reply, but she froze. Terror tightened her throat. "Close your door, Dottie. Now!"

Farris's mother frowned. "Why? I'm not cold at all."

"Hurry, Dottie."

Evidently, the urgency in India's voice penetrated. Dottie turned to grab the door handle and gasped. Because she saw what India had seen. An adult grizzly, some distance away, but ambling in their direction.

Because Dottie still hadn't finished the job, India reached across her and yanked the door shut. Then she closed her own and locked the car.

She wasn't foolish enough to believe they were safe. Everyone in this part of the world had seen pictures of what a bear could do to a car. Those four-inch claws could rip through metal if the animal was motivated.

Dottie seemed in shock. "But it's winter."

Dottie was right. It *was* winter. Which probably meant this was a black bear. Still a threat, but not as terrifying. Now that India could breathe, and now that the bear was closer, she cataloged the differences. No hump at its shoulders, and the shape of the face was wrong. Thank God.

"He must be a male black bear," she said. "They sometimes range around on nice days in the winter. I'm guessing he smelled our food."

"What should we do?" Dottie's tremulous question indicated her unease.

They were parked close to the edge of Farris's property. The bordering land was national forest. Aspenglow was in the middle of nowhere, which was part of its charm. "It's been a mild winter so far. He's probably hungry." Bears had an incredible sense of smell. "I think our only choice is to stay put."

"Honk the horn," Dottie said. "I saw Farris do that one time."

"Good idea." India gave several short toots. The bear paused, lifted his head, but kept coming. "If he's been in tourist areas scavenging, he may be habituated to humans. And not scared of us at all. I could try to drive away, but would that make him mad?" When India glanced at her passenger, Dottie's hands were clenched in her lap. Her face was pale. India fretted. Did stress worsen Dottie's heart condition?

The bear was on them now. He clambered up the hood of the car. India had been hoping he would abandon his exploration when he saw the two women. Apparently, he was not intimidated. Which probably meant he was accustomed to humans. If this had happened in a national park, the bear would be relocated.

Unfortunately, India and Dottie were on their own. Now the bear was on the roof of the car. He had to weigh four to five hundred pounds at least. Dottie yelped when the top of the car bulged slightly.

"Easy," India said.

"Can't we just toss our leftover food out the window?"

"Bad idea. Besides, I don't want to give him a chance to get into the car."

The bear slid back to the ground. He was on India's side now, his face pressed to the glass. Dottie shrieked.

Even though India knew they weren't really in too much danger, the whole experience sent adrenaline rushing through her bloodstream. "Go away," she yelled.

The bear snuffled and snorted. With one big swipe of his paw, he tore off the driver's-side mirror. Then India realized the problem. Not only was the bear *smelling* the food, she and Dottie had lined up the open containers all across the dash of the car. The bear could literally see the smorgasbord. And he wanted it.

"Start putting the food away," India whispered. "Stuff it all in the hamper. Maybe bears are like toddlers—out of sight, out of mind."

Dottie didn't waste any time. She shoved lids on plastic cups, gathered other items into zipper bags and tucked every bit of the picnic out of view.

India knew bears were smart. Clearly, their visitor could still smell the bounty. But she was hoping he would give up.

The bear must have been getting frustrated. He backed up two steps and flung himself at the window. The noise was incredible. A tiny crack appeared in the glass.

India had calmed down considerably, but now her

heart rate went back up. She honked the horn again. Yelled. The bear charged a second time.

Suddenly, a rifle shot rang out. The bear stopped, hung its head. Another rifle shot sounded closer. Whoever was shooting must not be trying to hit the bear. As far as India could tell, the shots were going over the animal's head.

A third shot sent the bear running.

Dottie grabbed India's hand. "Will he come back?"

India's unsteady laugh was weak at best. "Doesn't matter. We'll be gone." She started the engine and backed the car away from the water before turning around. There in front of them was a cowboy on a horse. His Stetson shadowed his face, but there was no doubt about his identity.

It was Farris. Farris had saved them.

Dottie—unbelievably, considering her health— bounded out of the car and ran to her son. "Thank God you came along." She flung her arms around Farris after he dismounted.

India followed more slowly, keeping an eye out behind her for the bear's possible return. "We're glad to see *you*," she said. The words were supposed to be light and amused. Instead, they came out sounding breathless. Her heart still raced. The aftermath of the incident had left her rattled.

She didn't think they had been in any real danger. But the incident was unnerving, to say the least.

Farris shot her a look. "You okay, Inkie?"

She nodded, suddenly unable to speak because her throat was tight with tears. It was such a frustrating, *girlie* response.

He must have understood her mental state. His smile was lopsided. "A bear encounter can be shocking for anybody. You were brave, both of you."

Dottie finally let go of her death grip on Farris's arm. "How did you know where we were?"

"I went by the house to grab something I forgot this morning. The housekeeper told me about your picnic. I felt bad about not helping you with the picture project, so I thought I might join you for lunch."

India frowned. "But how did you know to bring a rifle?"

"One of my men told me they've been carrying fire-power all week. Evidently, bear activity in the area has taken an uptick because of the milder temperatures."

"Would have been nice to know," India muttered.

Farris had the gall to laugh. "Have you ever fired a shotgun?"

"No…but that's beside the point."

"Not to mention the fact that it wouldn't have done you much good closed up in the car."

Dottie patted his arm. "It was very scary. My heart was racing. We're awfully glad you came along, Farris. Aren't we, India?"

India managed a nod, but the whole incident had left her shaken. She was supposed to be looking out for Dottie. Today's encounter was far too much stimulation for a woman with a heart condition.

Farris urged his mother toward the car. "I'll follow you back to the house."

It was odd seeing Farris in the rearview mirror. Twelve hours ago—give or take—India had shared his bed. And if Farris was to be believed, he wanted her there tonight and every night India was in Wyoming.

At one time, that knowledge would have thrilled her. She would have taken it as proof that there was hope for their marriage after all. But now, all these years later, she was not so naive. Now she understood that a man could separate lust from love.

Farris had certainly done so. He had excised love and marriage from his life. All that was left was physical pleasure and satisfaction.

India was still confused about why he needed *her* for that. Farris was wealthy, charismatic, enigmatic, charming when he wanted to be. Oh, and handsome. She couldn't forget that one. In a room full of either rugged cowboys or billionaire entrepreneurs, he would stand out.

Back at the ranch house, Farris helped his mother out of the car. As they headed inside, India lingered to gather the remnants of the picnic. When she walked into the kitchen to dump the trash and put a few things in the fridge, she found Farris waiting for her.

"Where's Dottie?" she asked. India avoided looking at him while she went about doing her few chores.

"She says she's going to take a nap, and that she might skip dinner."

"Oh."

Farris leaned against the counter with his arms folded across his chest.

India immediately felt guilty. "I'm so sorry," she said. "The picnic was my idea. But I never meant to put Dottie in danger."

He reached out and dragged her into his arms. "Don't

be ridiculous. You could have had that same meal in that same place a hundred times and never encountered a bear. The important thing is that you're both okay. To be honest, seeing that bear on the car with you two inside scared me, too."

India burrowed against his chest, drawing comfort from his embrace. "I realized pretty quickly that he wasn't a grizzly, but it was still frightening. I've never been happier to hear a rifle shot and to see you."

She felt his chest move as he chuckled. "Well, that's progress. Maybe I should thank that bear."

India decided she could stay in this spot for a very long time. Farris stroked her hair, his big hand warm and comforting on the back of her head. Letting him care for her was seductively appealing. She considered herself a strong woman. Even so, the knowledge that Farris would look out for her gave her a twinge of happiness deep inside.

They were standing so close together it was impossible for her to ignore the moment he became aroused. His sex pressed against her belly, thick and urgent. Even the stance of his body changed.

Before, he had been holding her to offer reassurance. Now his large frame vibrated with sexual energy. Every moment of last night's madness came rushing back, swirling about them like a cloud of temptation and threatening to drag them beneath the dangerous, unpredictable undertow.

What India *wanted* was to stay exactly where she was. Forever. Instead, she forced herself to take a step backward...literally.

"I should go," she said, not able to meet his gaze. "I should check on Dottie…see if she is okay."

"Don't," Farris muttered. "Don't go, Inkie." He reached for her hand and pulled her back into his orbit. He tunneled his fingers in her hair and tilted her head. His lips found hers unerringly.

India was lost. She forgot that it was day and not night. She forgot that the housekeeper was somewhere nearby. She forgot that Dottie could walk in at any second.

Farris's kiss was so unfair. It encompassed longing and tenderness. But also, lustful desperation. How was she supposed to withstand the double-edged assault?

He held her loosely. She could walk away easily. Yet she was trapped, trapped by her own need for this complicated, frustrating puzzle of a man.

His lips coaxed hers into parting, letting his tongue slide against hers. Desire curled in the pit of her belly. She inhaled the scents that were uniquely Farris, knowing she could pick him out in a dark room with her eyes closed.

He was her husband. Or he had been. She knew him intimately. His likes. His dislikes. Especially the ways to drive him wild in bed.

But what did any of that matter if the biggest secret of all was the one she could never fathom? Farris had ended their marriage, and she didn't know why.

Remembering the pain his decision had caused finally gave her the courage to break free of his spell. "No," she whispered. "No…" When she put her hands on his chest and shoved, he released her immediately.

India's timing was fortuitous. A noise in the hallway signaled the housekeeper's return. Farris's jaw was taut, his gaze stormy. "I won't apologize for wanting you," he said.

"I never asked you to. I wanted that kiss as much as you did."

Eight

India had plenty of hours to regret her too-honest statement. Why hadn't she said *I don't want this. I don't want you*? Probably because she wasn't that good an actress. She'd been plastered against Farris's chest, kissing him back like they were the last two people on a sinking ship.

He *knew* she wanted him. How was she going to stay out of his bed?

Going back to New York wasn't an option. Dottie genuinely needed companionship. Because of the relationship between the two women, India was bound by her compassion and her love to stay right here in this house.

Even though the legal bond between husband and wife had been severed, India still regarded Dottie as family. The "ex" part wasn't relevant. Her affection for the older woman was unchanged. Family bonds weren't so easily broken. And as India had come to understand since traveling to Wyoming, neither were the vows between husband and wife.

With Dottie hibernating after her harrowing experience and Farris out riding the range somewhere, India found herself at loose ends. Though the day was temperate for January, she had no desire at all to venture out alone. She would need some time to get over the bear incident.

In the end, she settled in the great room to work through more of the pictures. Even without Dottie present, India could organize envelopes by date and make sure the contents were in the right place.

It was nothing more than rabid curiosity and self-indulgence that led her to the oldest of the old pictures. India was fascinated by the images of a tiny Farris. In one photo, he was trying to blow out two candles on a cake with circus animals.

India's womb clenched with unexpected longing. She had assumed from the beginning that she and Farris would have babies. During the first year of their marriage, she had often daydreamed about being pregnant. She wanted a large family. A shrink would say it was because of all she had lost, and maybe that was true.

Farris hadn't been in a hurry for fatherhood. He'd said he wanted the two of them to enjoy each other for a few years. To travel. To grow closer.

It was hard to argue with that logic. But by the time India knew for certain she was ready, the marriage unraveled.

If things had gone differently at any point, India might have had a kindergarten-age son or daughter right now. It was almost impossible to imagine.

She made it all the way to the depths of one of the biggest boxes. A couple of empty file folders lined the bottom. But there was something underneath.

India removed the folders and found one last envelope. According to the information printed on the outside, this roll of film had been developed years ago at a facility no longer in business.

The envelope itself was old and torn at the edges. Did Dottie remember it was here, or had she hidden it away, because she didn't want to look at it?

Something about the envelope seemed sinister—which was melodramatic, of course. Maybe India was still edgy after the earlier bear trauma. Telling herself she was being stupid, she opened the old envelope and pulled out the stack of black-and-white photos. Her stomach sank to her toes.

There was a man in these shots, front and center. And he was holding his young son. This must be the infamous bigamist. India knew nothing about the dreadful person. She knew now that Dottie had changed her last name and Farris's to Quinn years ago. Farris's mother had wanted nothing to do with the husband who'd lied to her and deceived her.

Though India's stomach churned, there was no way in the world for her to simply set the photos aside. She was obsessed with them.

Suddenly, she flipped the package over to the front… where the address was. There was Dottie's name, but the line said Dorothy *Simpson. Farris Simpson.* Did he know? Had his mother ever told him the truth, or had they never talked about it?

If Farris was four when Dottie discovered the two-family charade, maybe little Farris eventually forgot he'd had another last name. Was that possible? He was a smart kid. Even at that age, surely Dottie would have had to give him an appropriate explanation for why they were moving out.

Obviously, the adult Farris knew what his biological father had done. But had Dottie kept the name a secret all these years? Had Farris ever demanded the information? Had he wanted to confront his father as an adult?

Or—like this envelope—had the family secrets been hidden and never again probed? The Farris she knew would not have forgiven such a terrible crime against his mother. He was so protective of Dottie. Surely, he would have thought about destroying the man who had ruined *his* life and his mother's.

Despite the passage of months and years, she felt foolish. How had she not known these things about her own husband?

Suddenly, the photos in India's hand felt like a ticking time bomb. She could put the envelope back where she'd found it and cover it with all the other packages she had removed from the box. The problem with that scenario was, sooner or later, Dottie would get to the bottom of the box.

India didn't want Dottie to be upset if she'd forgotten those pictures were there. India knew why they hadn't been thrown away. No mother could bring herself to destroy irreplaceable pictures of her beloved young child, even if the devil himself was in those same images.

Carefully, India looked at the photos one by one. Although it was impossible to judge a man's character by an old monochrome image, India decided on the spot that she didn't like him. Even holding Farris in his arms, Dottie's ex-husband seemed slimy.

He was playing house with one wife and son while having another family elsewhere. That was sick and twisted.

Why hadn't Dottie pursued legal action? Possibly because she had no financial resources without her husband.

The photos themselves made India uncomfortable. There were many of father and son, presumably at this long-ago birthday celebration. But there were also several of husband, wife and child. Dottie looked happy and proud, having no inkling of what was to come.

India's heart winced in sympathy.

Eventually, she put all the pictures back in the envelope, still unsure what to do about them. She could ask Farris's advice. He knew his mother better than anyone. But somehow, India couldn't imagine initiating that conversation. Farris's jaw would tighten, his blue eyes would flash fire, and what then?

India wanted to know whether or not to let Dottie come across the photos at all. Would the shock of discovering the old envelope be detrimental to her health? But if Dottie knew the pictures were there in the box all along and expected to find them, how would she react if they were gone?

What a tangle. India wished fervently that she had never attempted this task without Dottie. She hadn't been snooping. But the end result was the same. She had found out things she didn't want to know.

And then an even worse thought occurred to India. If she went to Farris and asked for his advice, she ran the risk of giving him a piece of information that Dottie might have been hiding for more than three decades.

If Farris didn't know his original surname, India would be handing him ammunition.

Good grief. How did something as seemingly innocent as organizing photographs turn into a potential crisis?

In the end, she tucked the envelope inside her sweater and sneaked back to her room, hoping Farris was still occupied out on the ranch. She tried to read a book she had brought with her from New York, but though it was a bestseller, it didn't keep her attention. Too many thoughts occupied her mind.

When her phone dinged around five, signaling a text, she picked it up with trepidation. Farris's name on the screen made her heart race…

Wear something nice for dinner. It's just you and me. We'll celebrate not getting eaten by a bear. :)

The text was remarkably lighthearted, coming from Farris.

What about Dottie?

She's having a tray in her room.

Is she okay?

She's great. Wants to watch TV. See you at six?

India smiled. I'll be there.

What exactly did "nice" mean? When she and Farris were first married, they'd often dressed for dinner. It was fun and romantic to eat at an intimate table for two beside their apartment's fabulous plate-glass windows overlooking the skyscrapers of New York.

But Wyoming was a far cry from New York City.

Even though India's boxes of winter clothes had arrived, her closet was woefully incomplete. *Wear something nice?* She shifted hangers from side to side. Something inside her wanted to knock Farris on his ass. Show him what he had given up. She would need to go for sexy and sophisticated using what she had.

Her little black dress had seen a lot of wear over the last few years. The scooped neck, cap sleeves and slim skirt that ended at her knees were both feminine and flattering. With black kitten heels and jewelry, the outfit would definitely do.

The house was warm. She had no plans to go outside, so her choice would be suitable at a dinner *pour deux*.

She showered and washed her hair, blowing it out until it brushed her jaw in a silky fringe. Next, she applied eyeliner, shadow and a touch of blush. Her hazel eyes that sometimes changed color to match her clothing or her mood were dark with excitement.

By 5:45, the butterflies in her stomach had turned into an entire migration. She felt mildly nauseated and infinitely torn.

Only this morning she had told Farris unequivocally that she shouldn't sleep with him. Was she prescient when she said *shouldn't*? Maybe her subconscious was more honest than she was. If Farris was suggesting a fancy dinner, and India was wearing makeup, wasn't that code for sex afterward?

She couldn't decide if she was elated or terrified.

As a finishing touch, she added the necklace and earrings Farris had given her on their wedding day. The earrings were simple—though flawless—diamond studs. The necklace was an eighteen-inch platinum chain interspersed with diamond stations.

She had always loved the pieces, because they were simple enough to wear every day. Some women might sell them after a divorce or stuff them in the back of a jewelry box. India had chosen to enjoy them despite what had happened.

Would Farris remember? Would he recall how he had surprised her? They had been in bed on their first night as a married couple. Farris made love to her with driving need and wild passion. In the aftermath, when they were both naked and breathless, he had reached under his pillow and produced two navy velvet boxes.

India had cried. Farris teased her gently as he put the necklace around her throat and helped her with the earrings. Then, of course, he made love to her again, this time with aching tenderness.

Now India stood in front of the mirror, absentmindedly stroking the chain with her fingertip. The woman in the mirror looked confused...torn. She had a great life in New York. Professionally and personally, she knew who she was in New York.

But now she was letting herself get sucked back into

a relationship that was a dead end. She wanted a home and family. Stability. Children.

Farris couldn't or wouldn't give her those things.

She stared at her reflection as if asking for direction, for advice. Was there any chance at all that Farris could be persuaded to revive their marriage?

And what about India? Did she desire that? Did she still love him?

She wanted to say no. He had hurt her so badly. He had damaged her confidence. His behavior had been inexcusable. Yet, last night, she had gone to his bed willingly, gladly.

She had grown and changed in the last five years. She was strong now. In charge of her own destiny. Surely, she wouldn't let Farris tear apart what she had built for herself.

If it weren't for Dottie, India would jump on the next plane. But without Dottie, there would be no reason for India to be here at all.

What a tangle…

At five minutes before six, she straightened her skirt, took one last look in the mirror and opened her door.

When she reached the dining room, wonderful smells wafted from the kitchen. Ivory candles burned with a muted glow. The polished oak table was beautifully set with handmade stoneware and heavy crystal goblets. Around the rim of each taupe-and-gray plate, a stylized wolf sprinted.

India didn't remember these dishes. But Farris had probably bought all sorts of things in the last five years. As she picked up a plate to look at the back, he appeared in the doorway. His cheeks were flushed, and his hair was mussed. "Hey," he said. His smile took the starch out of her knees.

"Hi," she said softly, feeling both awkward and happy. "Did you do all this?"

He snorted. "What do *you* think? The housekeeper prepared everything before I sent her home. My only job was to grill the steaks. They're almost done."

"Good. I'm starving."

He started to leave but lingered for a moment. "You look gorgeous, India. Luminous, actually."

"Thank you," she said. Had his eyes lingered on her jewelry and her bare legs? It was hard to tell. But the air between them was charged with *something*.

Farris was a feast for the eyes. He wore a bespoke suit, charcoal gray with a tiny black pinstripe. His crisp white shirt accented his golden skin. The navy-and-red tie knotted at his throat was no doubt as expensive as his Italian leather shoes. The metamorphosis was remarkable. From rugged cowboy to sophisticated business-man in the blink of an eye.

She started to tell him how amazingly handsome he was, but before she could get the words out, Farris glanced at the high-end watch on his wrist. "Oops," he said. "Gotta go. Don't want to ruin the main course."

He was back in less than five minutes, bearing a plat-ter of beautiful sizzling steaks. India helped him bring out the other dishes. There were twice-baked potatoes, sourdough bread and a broccoli-and-pea salad.

When they finally sat down at the table, India felt the awkwardness between them increase tenfold. Chewing and swallowing could only occupy a limited amount of time. In between, the silences grew.

Finally, she couldn't stand it any longer. She sipped her wine and cleared her throat. "You look very handsome yourself, Farris. I used to see you like this all the time. But more recently, I've come to know the cowboy version of you."

His lips quirked. "And which do you prefer?"

It was a fair question. "I'm not sure," she said. "The guy I first met was the suave businessman. But I've grown accustomed to the man on the horse."

"Grown accustomed?" He wrinkled his nose. "Hardly a glowing testimonial."

She cocked her head, staring at him. "Are you fishing for compliments? You must know that females everywhere have always found you attractive."

Now he frowned. "I never looked at other women when I was with you. I was faithful to our wedding vows."

"There was a time I doubted you," she said. "When our marriage was falling apart. Your behavior was so odd, so cold. I was certain you had found someone else."

"I didn't," he said tersely.

She waited for a further explanation, but she should have known Farris wasn't going to give up his secrets so easily. "This topic is depressing," she said. "Let's move on."

He shrugged. "Gladly."

India was frustrated. Trying to pry the truth from Farris was as futile as attempting to move one of the Teton peaks. He and granite had a lot in common.

"How soon will you be traveling again?" she asked.

"Probably next week. I need to spend a day or two in LA. Not long."

"What's in LA?"

"A string of movie theaters I'm considering buying. They've been allowed to get dingy, and they've been poorly managed. A friend told me about them. The company is solid in spite of everything. I like to keep my holdings diversified."

"I remember that about you. In fact, I must have picked up your expertise by osmosis. I've been able to invest small amounts here and there. Enough to feel secure."

Farris set down his fork, his eyes blazing with strong emotion. "You'll always be secure, Inkie. Even though you refused a divorce settlement, I've been putting money in an account for you most of the time we've been separated. Ten thousand dollars a month for the last two years."

Her jaw dropped. There was something odd about that explanation, but she couldn't put her finger on it. "That's absurd. I won't take your money, Farris. I don't need it. I am not your wife. We aren't a couple. You have no responsibility for me at all."

"I'll get more wine," he said, ignoring her protests.

She fumed. When he returned, she blasted him. "I'm not the naive kid you married. I don't need a man to coddle me."

He set the wine bottle on the table and glared at her. "I have the money. It's no big deal."

"It's a very big deal, actually. It's insulting."

His expression darkened. "My being nice to you is insulting?"

Why was she so upset? Truthfully, Farris's streak of honor and generosity was admirable. But if he couldn't be honest with her about why their marriage had foundered on unseen rocks, she was not willing to accept his money, no matter how rich he was.

"Let me rephrase that," she said, inhaling and exhaling and reaching for calm. "I didn't marry you for your money, and I didn't divorce you for your money. I'd rather not have something like that between us. Friendship? Yes…maybe. But not a ledger sheet."

Farris exhaled, as well, his temper subsiding as quickly as it had blown up. "Well, I suppose it's a moot point. The money will always be there. One day, when you have kids, it could pay for college."

Farris watched as India shook her head. "Do you think it would be appropriate for you to educate another man's child?" she asked.

Her smile was gentle, noncombative. But the question cut him off at the knees. He had never thought of it that way. In his mind, he had been helping India.

Picturing that mystery man in Inkie's life, in her bed, scared and infuriated him. "Well, give it away, damn it," he said. "I don't care what you do." The money was his penance, his cash fine for screwing up.

India was still seated, her wide-eyed gaze watchful. He didn't want her dissecting his psyche. It made him feel raw.

Dessert waited in the kitchen, but he had lost his appetite. "I need to catch up on some work emails," he muttered. "I'm glad you joined me for dinner."

All he could think about was escaping. India was never going to trust him again unless he told her the truth. And that, he could not do. Which meant he was going to bed alone tonight.

Before he could reach the door to the hallway, India was on her feet. It hurt to look at her. On some women, black was a somber color. India glowed. And her legs, those long shapely legs…

When she grasped his arm, it halted his forward progress. He hung there, too tormented to stay, too mindful of her feminine touch to go.

She waited patiently until he turned to face her. "Except for the arguing," she said, "that was a very romantic dinner, Farris. I assumed you had something else in mind for later."

"There's dessert in the kitchen," he said gruffly. "I'm not hungry."

"I wasn't talking about dessert." She shook her head as if he was a slightly dim student. "I was talking about sex. Why else did I get dressed up for you?" She moved closer, twining her arms around his neck. "You look hot in that suit, Farris. Handsome, sexy…"

She pressed a soft kiss to his lips.

He froze, sensing danger. "Wasn't it only this morning that you told me we shouldn't have sex?"

Her smile was wry. "*Shouldn't.* It's in the same category as *we shouldn't drive fast, we shouldn't eat carbs, we shouldn't procrastinate.*"

"I've been known to do all those things."

She stroked his jawline, her touch like fire. "Well, there you go."

His heart hammered in his chest. "What changed your mind?"

India moved away from him and stared at the floor,

sighing. "I *wanted* to have sex with you all along. But I was weighing the pros and cons. We'll keep this from Dottie. That's a given. And we'll have no expectations on either side, no promises. Agreed?"

"Look at me, Inkie."

With reluctance in her posture, she lifted her head. Hazel eyes gazed at him with a mix of caution and vulnerability. He had hurt her so badly. He knew it. And he would have to live with that knowledge for the rest of his life.

He swallowed hard. "I agree to your terms, but I have one more. Swear to me you'll have no regrets."

She frowned. "How can I do that?"

"It's a choice. I want us both to give and receive pleasure. With affection. And maybe even that friendship you mentioned. But no regrets. Not this time. Can you promise me that? No matter what happens, tell me you'll enjoy having sex between us with no second thoughts and no remorse."

"That's asking a lot. Neither of us can see the future."

"It doesn't matter," he said stubbornly. "I'm asking you to choose happiness, to wallow in physical bliss."

Her lips twitched. "Bliss? I have to say, you've never lacked confidence."

"I'm not joking, India. Those are my terms."

She came to him then and took the knot of his tie in her hand, pulling his head down. "I agree to your terms, Mr. Quinn."

Nine

The kiss lasted for a very long time. Farris felt light-headed. He'd never dreamed she would actually agree. Even though they were clearly as sexually compatible as ever, he'd assumed India would hold the past against him.

Maybe she was more forgiving than he was, or maybe he'd been right earlier in the day. They were both lonely. And in bed, they were perfection.

He tucked her head against his shoulder and gathered her closer, running his hands down her back and cupping her heart-shaped ass. "I find it hard to breathe when you're around."

"Ditto," she said, the word muffled.

He eased back only enough to let her have oxygen.

"I didn't have time to shave earlier. What if I do that and come to your room in half an hour?"

Her thumb tested the late-day stubble on his chin. "I like it, Farris. It makes you look human."

What does that mean? "So…"

She took his hand, twining her fingers with his. "So, come to my room now. I want to undress you. Any objections?"

He sucked in a much-needed breath. "Not a single damn one." Her show of confidence delighted him and made his tongue feel thick. He wanted to be in control of the situation, but that wasn't in the cards.

In the alcove where both their doors were closed, he kissed her cheek. "Let me grab protection," he said. "Two minutes, tops."

India's dreamy smile faded, leaving her expression bleak. "It's not necessary. Last night I was feeling…" She trailed off, shrugging.

"Feeling what?"

She played with her necklace. "Uncertain. As I told you, I'm on the pill. And I trust that you're clean. We don't need the condoms."

Farris knew she didn't believe him when he said he hadn't been with other women. But at least she trusted him this much. "Okay," he said gruffly. He reached around her to open the guest room door. "Ladies first."

There was a single lamp burning on the dresser. The low-wattage bulb shed just the right amount of illumination for a tryst. India still held his hand. She sat down on the side of the bed. "I was timid with you in the beginning. Do you remember? I used to get embarrassed when you watched me undress at night."

His heart cracked. "I remember."

She unbuttoned his jacket and played with his belt buckle. "I'm not that woman anymore. I feel like I could devour you."

Dear Lord. When they walked into the room, he had been semierect. Now he was so hard he shuddered with it. "Feel free," he muttered.

When she bent her head to wrestle with his belt, Farris fixated on the nape of her neck—so innocent, so pure where the silky blond hair ended and the creamy white skin began. He stared at a spot on the ceiling, struggling for control.

Once India slithered the belt free and tossed it aside, he expected her to unzip him. Instead, she slid to the floor and began untying his shoes. When she touched his ankles to remove the shoes *and* the socks, she might as well have been touching his sex. That was how much it affected him.

She was kneeling to do her task. Once his feet were bare, she reached to unfasten his zipper. His knees locked. His throat dried. "India." He tried to swallow. "Could you hurry? Please."

When she looked up at him, her smile was smug. "Patience, cowboy." She slid her hands inside his dress pants and took them to the floor, along with his boxers. Sitting back on her heels, she commanded him. "Step out of those."

He obeyed her instruction, but it wasn't graceful. When he was bare from the waist down, India caressed each of his knees with a single fingertip and then stood. "Good boy," she whispered.

She kissed him at the exact same moment her fingers

wrapped around his erection. *Holy hell.* He put a hand behind her neck and dragged her lips to his. It was either a kiss or a duel—he couldn't decide. It sure as hell wasn't romantic.

India nipped his bottom lip with sharp teeth. He bit her tongue and sucked the tiny wound. They were both breathing like marathoners.

Though the kiss went on, India was still at work. Her slender fingers dealt with his tie. He jerked it free while his lover started in on his shirt buttons.

He resented the moment he had to let her go long enough to rip his arms out of the shirt and jacket and cast both aside.

In half a second, he was back with her again. He was starving for the taste of her. Her arms were around his neck now, near strangling him.

"Your clothes," he panted. "You still have on your clothes."

India kicked off her shoes. "It's only the dress," she said, her smile half mocking, half mischievous. "Nothing else."

There was a ringing in his ears. His chest heaved. Could it be true?

Carefully, he cupped one breast through the fabric of her dress. The curvy flesh and taut nipple were unfettered. *Damn.*

Suddenly, he couldn't wait another second. He pushed her back onto the bed, shoved her dress to her waist and mounted her with an aggression set free by his splintered control. "Tell me you want me," he growled. "Tell me."

She gasped when he thrust hard, all the way to her womb. "I want you, Farris. I want you."

The words inflamed him. He rode her hard, groaning when her legs went around his waist. "This will take the edge off, Inkie. Then all night I'm going to f—"

She put a hand over his mouth, halting the torrent of words. "No promises, remember? We're living in the moment."

Farris knew he hadn't made her come. He felt bad about it. But his body seized control and drove him toward completion. The end hit him hard. He wanted to say something to her. To tell her how he felt. But there was no time. Without protection, the sensation of being inside her was magnified.

He choked out her name, shuddered and emptied his essence into her welcoming body.

When it was over, he could hear his heart beating in his ears. His limbs were lax and weak.

India trembled in the aftermath. Farris's hunger was more than she'd expected. For the briefest moment, she pondered whether or not he might really have been celibate since their divorce. Then she mentally chided herself. Her ex-husband was a highly sexual creature, a masculine animal in his prime.

She knew his appetite for sex. There was no way he had stayed out of other women's beds. No way at all. To entertain that fantasy—even for a moment—would be opening herself up to unimaginable hurt.

Even so, her body sang with pleasure. Despite the lack of an orgasm, she knew Farris would make it up to her. The level of his arousal and desperation had singed her with fire. To know how badly he wanted her smoothed her bruised feelings.

The divorce had damaged her self-esteem. In the months afterward, she had questioned her desirability, her appeal. She had felt incredibly vulnerable.

Now, tonight, she knew the truth. Whatever else had happened, Farris hadn't lost interest in her body or in their sexual intimacy.

He stirred and laughed raggedly. "I'm sorry, Inkie."

She tunneled her fingers through his hair. "I'm sure you'll get to me eventually. I thought your urgency was flattering."

"Sarcasm?" He rolled to his feet and helped her up, grinning.

"Oh, yeah."

"Good news," he said, unzipping her dress and removing it with impressive speed before scooping her up in his arms.

Her cheek rested against his chest. "Oh?"

With one hand, he flipped back the covers. Gently, he deposited her in the center of the mattress. "Now it's all about you."

"Oh, my." She pretended to joke and flirt, but her heart hammered.

Farris joined her beneath the covers and sprawled on his side. "I hope I remember all the good spots."

"I'll help if you get lost."

After that, there was no time for humor. She was too busy grabbing handfuls of the sheet and trying to wring every drop of delight out of this delayed foreplay. She arched her back and panted.

Farris slid one hand between her thighs and bent to lick her nipple. "So far so good?" he asked, his voice muffled.

She groaned as heat spread through her belly. "Definitely."

He touched her lightly, teasingly. But she was so primed she knew her climax was imminent. She wanted this encounter to last.

When he entered her with two fingers and then three, she began to beg. Everything in her body focused on that one most sensitive spot. She was slick and needy, embarrassingly so. "Enough, Farris. I want you. Now."

He moved on top of her but didn't join their bodies. A lock of hair fell over his damp forehead. His cheeks were ruddy with color. His eyes glittered. For once, the granite jaw was softened with a smile.

"I've missed you, India." He kissed her on the forehead. "I forgot how exquisite you are, how beautiful. I'm going to watch you come. What do you say to that?" His gorgeous mouth tilted in a sensual twist of masculine lips.

In this situation, she would have preferred they come together. Now that Farris's immediate need was satisfied, he was capable of destroying her and witnessing every emotion on her face. "I'd rather you not."

He blinked. "Are you serious?"

"Yes," she said baldly. "We haven't been together in a long time. It will make me self-conscious."

"We were together last night."

"You know what I mean. I'm talking about our life before. Last night we were both desperate to scratch an itch. But you've already come once tonight, and now you're concentrating on me. It's too intense."

"Relax, India. I'm going to enjoy this as much as you are. I only have one smallish request."

His thumb still moved lazily against the center of her sex, where every nerve was poised to explode.

"Request?" The word came out choked.

"I want you to keep your eyes open the entire time. I want you to look at me when I make you come. I want to see every expression on your face."

She was so close to climax she wanted to curse at him. Her hips shifted restlessly. "Fine," she said.

Farris smiled, a sweet, totally un-Farris-like smile. "Thank you. Now spread your legs for me. As wide as you can."

His request sent another jolt of heat through her middle to stoke the slow burn. She caught her breath but obeyed. The simple act of sliding her feet across the soft sheet made her blush.

"Good girl." Farris took his time looking her over.

Her nipples were so hard and tight they ached. Her chest rose and fell rapidly with her jerky breathing.

He put both hands on her thighs, massaging the tender flesh on the inside with a firm touch. Next, he slid his hands higher, high enough for him to part her labia with his thumbs. "Your sex is stunning, India. Rosy and hot and so incredibly appealing."

When he bent to brush his tongue across her folds, she cried out.

Farris pulled back. "You don't like that?"

She called him a name that made him laugh. He used his thumbs again. She felt open, so open. As if her body was one yearning, empty vessel inviting him to seize and plunder. Need clawed and built inside her.

"Do you want to come, my sweet?" His gaze was devilish.

"You know I do." He had a single fingertip where she needed it most. If he pressed down just a millimeter more, she could…

Before she could divine his intent, he stroked her twice with devastating effect. Her orgasm crashed through her, riding a wave that was the cusp of pain and pleasure. In the end, she screamed his name after all, unable to bear the incredible physical release. Before she had finished the final slide, Farris entered her again.

He filled her, worshipped her, whispered words of praise and carnal threat.

India trembled, feeling the want build once more.

Farris was gentler this time, but no less focused. He thrust hard and then easy, coaxing her to join him on this next ride, setting up a seductive ebb and flow she couldn't resist.

She didn't think it was possible, but soon, her body responded to his. He rolled to his back, putting her on top. Now he played with her breasts.

His chest heaved, his breathing no steadier than hers.

The gleam in his eyes was a challenge. India found her rhythm, taking charge of the dance. She leaned forward to rest her palms on his shoulders.

Farris groaned out her name. "You haven't lost your touch, Inkie."

"Nor you, cowboy." As she looked down at him, her heart squeezed hard. The truth was a bitter pill. She still loved him. Tears burned the backs of her eyes. She blinked them away angrily. No way in hell would she let him see what he had done to her…what he was doing to her again. She rotated her hips. "How does it feel to wait, Farris? Not so easy, is it?"

Now the granite jaw was back. He took control in an instant, rolling her to her back and taking what he wanted. "Nothing about you and me was ever easy," he muttered.

His raw statement shook her. Even as her body responded to his expert touch, her heart wept. What was she doing?

When she was silent, Farris buried his face in her neck. "Don't cry, Inkie, please. You're killing me."

She hadn't even realized that a tear or two had escaped, running down her cheeks and into her hair. "I'm not," she lied.

Farris slowed his wild motions. His big body trembled over hers. "I'm sorry, India. Sorry I hurt you so badly."

"Empty apologies don't interest me," she said, her words blunt and not at all diplomatic in her pain. "You made our marriage impossible. You made *us* impossible. I'll never forgive you for that."

His gaze went blank, every emotion wiped away. All that remained was lust and domination. He took her again and again until she finally cried out in a second climax. Only then did he let himself come.

If tonight was a competition, Farris won.

They were as close as two people could be physically, but the chasm between them had widened. Turned out, sex for the sake of loneliness wasn't so great when it was all over.

India wished desperately that they had been in Farris's room. Then she could have walked out and shut the door behind her.

As it was, Farris was *here*. Big and warm and naked. And possibly half-asleep.

Now that the sexual insanity was over, her skin chilled. In their madness, they had thrown the covers aside. Even with Farris still half on top of her, she was cold.

When she shivered hard, Farris reared up on one hand and touched her shoulder. "Good Lord, India. Your skin is like ice." He dragged the covers into place and then visited her bathroom. When he returned, he looked down at her, frowning. "You're still not warm, are you?"

She shook her head. "No. But it doesn't matter. I'll put on some pajamas when you leave." As hints went, it was pretty clunky and obvious.

Farris didn't seem to notice. He crawled under the covers and spooned her. "Don't be sad," he whispered. The words tickled her ear. His strong arms enfolded her in blissful heat. In fact, his whole body encompassed hers. She could tell he was hard again, though he made no move to continue where they had left off.

"I'm not sad." Again, she lied. "You gave me two orgasms," she said, pretending to be smug. "How could anything be wrong?"

When she heard Farris's regular breathing, she sneaked a glance at the clock on the bedside table. It was late, very late. How was she supposed to oust the man of the house from her bed? After all, this was technically his bed, too. He owned it all.

But he didn't own India.

She dozed on and off, drifting in a blissful place where reality faded and her marriage still existed, intact and perfect. She must have still been dreaming when a warm, masculine hand cupped her breast and toyed with her nipple.

Moving restlessly, she made a choked sound of pleasure and placed her hand over his. "I'm tired," she said, the words laced with petulance. Was she really? Or was she punishing him?

Farris nuzzled the sensitive skin beneath her ear. Licking. Biting her earlobe.

India gasped as heat sparked in her veins. This was her chance. She could sit up, exit the bed, prove to both of them that she didn't need this. She didn't need him.

But the lure of drugged, liquid pleasure was impossible to resist. *Drugged?* Was that the right word? She was stone-cold sober. Yet she felt high, addicted to Farris.

Before she could process his intent, he had eased her onto her back. In one long-fingered hand, he trapped both her wrists and lifted them over her head.

His eyes were dark cobalt. The sizzle she felt in her bloodstream must have been ignited by the tiny flame in his pupils. He looked nothing like the suave businessman or even the easygoing cowboy.

Tonight, India's ex-husband was a pirate, a seducer of innocent women. An irresistible bad boy.

She struggled against his grip. "Let me go," she said indignantly. But the words held little heat.

Farris cocked his head and smiled, his grin a flash of white in the shadowy room. "No."

"No?" She gaped at him.

"*Nyet. Nein.* Shall I go on?"

"You can't keep me here." The shiver that worked

its way down her spine had nothing to do with the temperature of the room.

Farris squeezed her wrists. "Can't I?" The power in his one large hand was apparent. "Try to get away, Inkie. I'm sure we'd both enjoy that."

The scenario he described made her heart race. Her mouth was dry. "Never mind. I'll stay. But I need a glass of water."

"Too bad. Rest time is over."

"Is that what we were doing? Resting?"

His chuckle made the hair on her arms stand up. "I was. Don't know about you." Despite his words, he handed her a tumbler. She took a sip and gave it back.

India scrunched up her nose, trying to decide if he was serious or if he was merely toying with her. "You never once tried anything kinky with me when we were married. I think you're bluffing."

"I never bluff." He reached toward the nightstand and picked up a tube of lotion. India used it on her hands at night. "This should work," he said.

"You're freaking me out." She wet her lips with the tip of her tongue. "What are you going to do with that?"

"Don't be so suspicious," he said gently. For a man with only one free hand at his disposal, he was remarkably deft. After uncapping the container, he squirted a thin line of white down the center of her rib cage and all the way to her navel. "Relax, India. You'll like this, I swear."

India wasn't sure what she'd thought he was going to do, but it wasn't this. Somehow, he had retrieved his necktie earlier when she wasn't looking. Now he quickly tied her wrists together and secured them to the headboard.

"Perfect," he said. "Close your eyes if it will make you feel better."

Ten

Farris hadn't set out to play sex games with India. It was an idea that had come to him while she was nestled in his arms with her butt cradling his erection.

The look on her face made him want to laugh out loud, but he stifled his amusement. It was much more satisfying to watch India try to decipher his intentions.

When she had nothing else to say, he knelt between her thighs, making sure to stretch her legs as far apart as possible, just for effect.

His lover was wide-eyed, her gaze filled with a combination of confusion and shock and disbelief.

The one thing Farris didn't see was reluctance. And he watched for it carefully. His goal was to bring pleasure to his lover. One negative response, and this interlude was over.

"Are you comfortable?" he asked.

She pouted. "What do *you* think?"

He wished she could see herself. Her body was sensual and abandoned in this pose, like a concubine waiting to be chosen.

Farris leaned forward. Balancing himself on one hand, he used his other hand to massage India's chest, spreading the slightly fragrant lotion from breast to breast and back again. When her breath caught audibly, he knew his captive was enjoying herself.

"This is good lotion," he said, the words prosaic. "I like the way your skin absorbs it." Without warning, he concentrated on her nipples, working the cream around and around until it disappeared.

India shuddered and moaned.

Next, he moved down to her flat belly. She was ticklish. He would have to be careful. With the flat of his palm, he massaged her stomach, dipping occasionally into her navel. "How does that feel?"

There was no answer but an inarticulate sound that suggested she was as aroused as he was. He leaned over to kiss her. "I like pleasuring you, Inkie."

He gave her no warning for what happened next. Quickly, he dispensed lotion right onto the tiny nub where all her pleasure centers coalesced. "Come for me, lovely girl."

With light, purposeful strokes, he made her shatter. Her hips arched off the bed, and her eyelids flew open. "Farris."

Clumsily, he untied her and then entered her with a groan. "I want you, India. All night. Remember?"

He went a little crazy at that point. Exhaustion and

driving lust made him loopy. He couldn't believe he was making love to her again. He couldn't explain how that made him feel. Elated and invincible. But he deliberately shoved away thoughts of the future.

Nothing mattered but this bed in this room for this night.

Afterward, they really did sleep. But only in snatches. Every time he awakened, he needed her again. Sometimes it was sweet and slow. At others, the dark side beckoned, and they drove each other to the brink.

As dawn broke, he rolled over and yawned. "I need to go to my room. The housekeeper will be here soon. And it would be just like Dottie to make this the one morning she decides to be an early riser."

India nodded sleepily. "Yes." She squeezed his hand.

With great reluctance, he rolled out of bed and donned his wrinkled clothes, minus the dinner jacket. India watched him as he dressed. Which meant that he was soon hard again. He eased up the zipper on his pants gingerly. "Will I see you at breakfast?" he asked.

"Unless I fall into a sleep coma, yes. But since my stomach is already growling, I plan to show up."

"Good. I don't want you to get cold again. Let me wrap this around your shoulders." He picked up the fluffy woven blanket that had been neatly folded on the bench at the foot of the bed. After tucking it around India to his satisfaction, he kissed her one last time. When he stepped back, he noticed something else on the bench. "What's this?"

It was mostly a rhetorical question. He recognized the faded yellow envelope as one of the many batches of photos his mother had shipped from New York. His limbs weakened and his blood went icy as he processed the information written on the outside.

"Where did you get this?" he asked hoarsely. "Why do you have it? And why was it hidden under that blanket?"

India sat up, clutching the fuzzy blanket to her chest. "I can explain."

His head felt funny. "Please do."

"I was maybe going to ask your advice."

"That sounds remarkably convenient, as explanations go…" He heard the cutting sarcasm in his tone. India went white. But hell, *he* was the one who should be upset. And he would have been, if his emotions hadn't been encased in ice.

"It's true," she said. "I was digging through one of Dottie's boxes, trying to sort the envelopes by date. When I got to the bottom of the box, there were a couple of empty file folders. That one set of pictures was underneath. I didn't want Dottie to find it unexpectedly and be upset. But then I wondered if she had hidden the photos deliberately."

"Why would she be upset?"

India frowned. "Don't play dumb with me. You see the date. I found pictures of your father in there."

"I don't have a father." He removed the stack of black-and-white photos. Flipping through them made his stomach churn with nausea. "No worries," he said curtly. "I'll burn these."

"No," India protested. "I don't think you should. Obviously, she kept them because of you. She wanted images of you to remember."

Suddenly, something hit him. "You said maybe... Why *maybe*?"

India's gaze was haunted. "Your mother's married name is on the envelope. I thought she might have hidden that information from you."

He frowned. "You thought I didn't know the name I was born with?"

"You were little. It occurred to me that when Dottie had your names changed, she might have concealed your birth name."

"I may have been small, India, but I can assure you I knew my name. And I didn't forget it. How could I? It's on my birth certificate." He paused, struggling to juggle the emotions duking it out in his chest. "I hate Simpson to the depths of my soul. He made my mother have a baby out of wedlock. Do you know what that did to her? She thought she was married, but she wasn't. And thus I am a bastard."

"Nobody cares about stuff like that anymore, do they?"

"Perhaps not. But it mattered to my mother. It matters even now. She was conned into having an illegitimate child."

"I'm so sorry, Farris."

India's sympathy was like acid on his raw emotions. Especially since Farris possessed information India did not. He stuffed the pictures back into the envelope.

"Give it to me," she said. "I'll talk to Dottie about the pictures."

His fingers gripped the packet until his knuckles turned white. "I don't want to see myself with him."

"You won't have to. I'll take it. But you can't destroy the photos without Dottie's permission."

He knew what India said was true. But rage boiled inside him, corroding his morality, destroying his peace of mind. *Fuck* morality. He wanted these photographs out of his house. Now.

India climbed out of bed, her body concealed in the soft blanket. When she came closer, he flinched. "Stay away from me," he said curtly.

"Hand them over, Farris. Please."

In the end, she had to tug the envelope from his nerveless fingers. She tucked the pictures in a dresser drawer and returned to where he stood. She put a hand on his arm. "Come back to bed," she said softly. "Let me hold you."

He allowed her to pull him, only because he had lost his way. He had no father, no wife, only years of regret. Seeing those damn photos sent him back to the time when he had been a confused, hurting boy…powerless… devastated. He hated that boy. He hated being helpless. He had spent years constructing his armor, refusing to let anyone or anything get too close.

India had been the only person he'd allowed himself to care about, besides his mother. But he had screwed that up beyond repair. *Failure. Failure.*

Beneath the covers, *she* spooned *him* this time, stroking his hair, whispering words of encouragement and comfort. Nothing penetrated his fog of pain and confusion, nothing except the sound of her voice.

His aching body felt much like the time he had come home from work with the flu. Dottie had been out of town. Farris and India were already divorced. Farris had holed up in his New York apartment, bedridden, for seventy-two hours. Solitary. Bereft.

He had shivered and slept fitfully, barely managing to take medicine and drink liquids. It was the most alone he had ever felt in his life.

Now, even though he ached all over, there was something different. India offered peace. He closed his eyes and pretended the last five years hadn't happened. Hell, while he was at it, he pretended that his father was a gentle giant of a man who loved playing catch with his son and didn't have another family stashed away somewhere, a *legal* family.

India was singing to him now, soft ballads that he used to play for her on the guitar. Her voice was low and sweet, even when the melody was not quite in tune. When was the last time he had picked up his guitar? The beautiful instrument India had given him for their second anniversary brought back too many memories.

He drifted, half awake, half asleep, reluctant to leave this place of warmth and absolution. But, gradually, he came out of his funk. "I should go," he said, hoping she would argue with that.

"Yes. It's late."

He sat up on the side of the bed, feeling foolish and uncertain. No other person had ever seen him at such a low point. Some part of him was angry that India had been the one to witness his crisis. He had spent an entire night demonstrating his masculinity. They had made love with passion and insanity.

Now would she regard him as a figure of pity?

When he forced his limbs to move, to stand his body upright, his head spun. He had to put a hand on the dresser to steady himself. "I'm sorry about all that," he said gruffly.

India lay on her side, head on her hand, eyes watchful. "We all have our moments, Farris. I think you probably came by yours honestly. Being lied to is painful."

Was that a dig? Did she mean to point out that she had suffered, too...because of Farris's lies? But he hadn't lied to her. He had rationalized this subject a million times. Withholding information wasn't the same as lying.

He crossed the room to the door, holding his jacket in his hand. The distance felt like a hundred miles. As he prepared to leave her, he opened his mouth to say something, though he didn't know what. In the end, he simply slipped out, leaving India behind. It was for the best.

India made it to breakfast. Farris did not.

Dottie assured her that she had seen her son in passing. "He grabbed a cup of coffee and headed out. Said he had overslept. That doesn't sound like him. And I don't think he looked well. I hope he isn't coming down with something."

India made a noncommittal response and helped herself to eggs, bacon and toast. "The question is," she said, "how are *you* doing, Dottie? Have you recovered from our excitement yesterday?"

"Oh, pooh," Dottie said. "A little thing like that can't get me down. I wish I had gotten a picture, though. It would have made a great social media post."

"True," India said, laughing.

After breakfast, India wasn't surprised when Dottie wanted to work on the photo albums again. In truth, they hadn't placed a single photo yet. They were still working on the sorting and discarding.

India knew this was her chance to talk to Dottie. If she waited, she might chicken out. "I want to brush my teeth and grab a sweater," she said. "Meet you in the great room in fifteen minutes?"

"Of course."

The morning passed slowly. India tried to hide her frequent yawns. Her eyes were gritty from lack of sleep. She used the sweater she had brought as concealment for the pictures she'd found.

Finally, she worked up the courage to broach the subject that had sent Farris into a tailspin. "Dottie?"

"Hmm?" Farris's mother didn't even look up. She had two stacks of pictures in her hands and was trying to put them in order and ditch duplicates.

India tried a second time. "Dottie. I need to tell you something." Her voice got husky at the end. Was she afraid or embarrassed to talk about the taboo subject?

Dottie must have heard the emotion in India's words. Her head snapped around. "What's wrong, love?"

"Um…" India felt her cheeks get hot and her stomach tighten. "I came in here yesterday afternoon. Decided to put more envelopes in order." She pointed. "In that box over there, I found something at the bottom… an envelope that's older than all the rest. It was hidden under some file folders. I didn't know if you remembered putting it there."

Dottie froze. "Where is it?"

India reached for her sweater. "Right here. I didn't want to upset you."

Farris's mother pulled the photos out of the creased

envelope that was more than three decades old. "Oh, yes," she said. "I remember these well."

She flipped through the black-and-whites one at a time, her eyes glassy with tears. "He was such a precious boy. So handsome. Sweet and kind."

"Farris wanted to burn them when he found them in my bedroom."

Dottie jerked. She stared at India. "What was Farris doing in your bedroom?"

Oh, crap. India stuttered as her face flamed.

Dorothy Quinn shook her head slowly, a small smile replacing the sadness that had cloaked her moments before. "Don't answer that, sweetheart. None of my business. But thank you for saving these. I don't have any earlier than this."

India frowned. "Why not?"

"When I left the house of the man I called my husband, I was only able to take Farris and two small suitcases, the bare necessities. When Simpson realized I was not coming back, he flew into a rage. He called me—drunk and screaming—told me he had tossed the baby book and all the baby pictures into the fireplace." She paused, the memories painting her features with grief.

"Oh, my God. I am so sorry, Dottie."

She shrugged. "I think he was trying to erase my boy. But it's okay. I still have Farris, and that's what matters."

"I didn't mean for him to see the pictures," India said. "I thought you might have hidden the name from him so he wouldn't do something foolish as he grew up. But Farris told me he knew his name and never forgot."

"Your theory isn't so far-fetched. Farris carried an unbearable burden of anger. When I had the financial means, I took him to a counselor who specialized in childhood trauma. It was twice a week for six months. That's all I could afford."

"Did it help?"

"I like to think so. He was calmer after those sessions concluded, better able to manage his emotions. But the fact remained—Farris was robbed of a normal father/son relationship, and nothing I did was ever going to make up for that."

India was silent for a moment. "What about you, Dottie? Who helped you with your anger?"

The older woman winced, as if remembering. "I had to lock *all* my grief and anger into a big box and bury it. My son was my responsibility. It was only after Farris finished college and moved out on his own that I let my guard down. I was fortunate to find an excellent therapist. Actually, he's more of an old friend now. I still see him when I'm in the city. I'm a work in progress, as they say. But I did finally let go of the anger. If not, I would have died long before now."

"I hear something in your voice when you speak of him. Is this man something more to you than a shrink?"

Dottie blushed. "Herman can't date a patient, and I won't end our working relationship. So we do what we do."

"Have you ever wanted more?"

"Of course I have, but I've never had the courage to try. I made such a huge mess of my life, India. A mistake like that stays with you. The fear of another misstep, trusting another con man, is a powerful deterrent."

"I understand." But what India really understood was that Dottie and Farris had suffered terribly and now deserved to be happy. Was there no way forward for them? She shook her head slowly. "Well, if you and Farris have both seen those photos, and we know they're the oldest ones, we might as well start the first album."

Dottie bounced and clapped her hands. "Oh, goodie."

Her childlike delight made India smile. Soon, several pages were filled, pages documenting a young, innocent Farris. And Dottie, of course.

Eventually, India's stomach growled. "I think we deserve a break." She wasn't actually hungry, but she wanted desperately to check on Farris. She wasn't sure he was okay. The man who'd walked out of her bedroom this morning had looked shell-shocked. She had fallen asleep again after he left, but her dreams had been unsettled.

When she and Dottie made it to the dining room for lunch, there were only two places set. That wasn't entirely unusual midday. But the housekeeper burst India's bubble. The woman addressed Dottie. "Mr. Quinn wanted me to tell you that there was an emergency out on the ranch. One of the men got a bad cut. Mr. Quinn took him into town to the ER, and he's catching an earlier flight to LA."

Dottie nodded. "Thank you. I'm sure he'll call later."

India was stunned and hurt. Farris had mentioned going to LA *next week*. Now, suddenly, he was on a plane? That was a remarkably fast change of plans.

In the course of the next half hour, she ate enough of her meal not to make a scene, but she excused herself soon after. In her room, she stared at the bed where she and Farris had spent their wild night. Apparently, while India and Dottie had been in the great room this morning tackling their project, the housekeeper had changed the sheets.

India sat down on the bench at the end of the bed and put her face in her hands. Farris had asked for no regrets. But she had plenty already.

She had to leave Wyoming. She couldn't do this. If she got so upset because she wanted to inhale her lover's scent on the sheets—and now those sheets were gone—how would she survive the moment when she had to say goodbye to Farris a second time in her life? Making love to him and thinking she could keep her heart intact was stupid.

As she sat there, remembering every intimate, sensual, deeply satisfying moment of the night before, she realized there was only one possible solution. As soon as Farris returned to Aspenglow, India would have to confront him.

The thought made her stomach churn with dread. She wasn't good at confrontation, particularly with Farris. But her life was stuck. She needed closure, even if that word had become trite from overuse. Until she knew why he had ended their marriage, she would always wonder. She would always second-guess herself and her decisions.

Emotional upheaval made the walls begin to close in. She had to get out of this house. Dottie usually rested at this time. India scribbled a brief note and slid it under her mother-in-law's door.

Then she bundled up in her warmest clothes and headed for the barn. She wasn't an extremely experienced rider, but she could handle a gentle horse. She had noticed the other day a stall marked *Daisy*. Sure enough, when she explored the depths of the massive barn, she found that Farris had kept the gentle, slow mare that had been India's.

"Hey there, old girl. Do you remember me?"

The horse's gentle whinny sounded like a yes. India found the same saddle she had used when she was married to Farris. Hefting it off the nail and settling it on Daisy's back seemed like old times. The motions came back to her, a skill back-burnered but never forgotten.

When she had checked all the buckles and tightened the cinches, she led Daisy outside. The day was cloudy and in the low thirties. India wouldn't freeze if she took a gentle ramble around the ranch.

When she mounted the agreeable mare, she exhaled, determined not to think about Farris once this afternoon.

Unfortunately, everything about the ranch recalled her ex-husband's presence. Aspenglow bore his stamp in each fence post and blade of grass.

She tried anyway.

Gradually, the crisp air and striking scenery calmed her spirit.

Thoughts spun through her brain and disappeared like wisps of clouds. She let them go, knowing that this time away from the ranch house was a buffer she desperately needed. Farris had commandeered even her dreams.

That had to stop.

Self-reflection was a bitch. She was forced to admit to herself that she had been spinning a narrative where

Farris discovered he couldn't live without her. It was a dangerous fiction.

He had spoken truth. When India described their relationship as two lonely adults looking for comfort, Farris had agreed.

What was the worst that could happen if India demanded an explanation for the cold war five years ago? In the first place, Dottie might inadvertently get caught in the cross fire. That would be bad. But India could take precautions. Secondly, Farris might stonewall India. That would make her furious. She would have no recourse but to leave and abandon Dottie. Not a good outcome. And last of all, there was the remote possibility that Farris might finally tell India the truth.

Thinking about that made her both hopeful and terrified. Did she really want to know? After all this time?

Maybe deep down, she didn't.

But like nasty medicine, discovering the truth about her disastrous marriage was the only thing that would set her free.

Eleven

India rode the perimeter for two hours, maybe longer. She deliberately didn't look at her watch or her phone. She needed peace and silence to clear her head.

By following the fence line at a lazy pace, she was assured of not getting lost. She might be desperate for answers, but she wasn't foolhardy.

Eventually, she intersected the small dirt road that led back to the bunkhouse. She wasn't quite ready to return home. Her explorations, both literal and mental, had energized her. So, she passed the road and kept following the fence. Just a mile or two more, and she would turn around. She didn't want to miss dinner, and she definitely didn't want to alarm Dottie.

Disaster hit without warning. A prairie dog popped

its head out of a hole right as Daisy ambled by. Startled, the usually docile mare reared up on her hind legs.

India had gotten comfortable during her slow ride. She hadn't been holding the reins as tightly as she should. Even worse, she was not a skilled enough rider to take control of the situation.

It was like witnessing herself in slow motion. She yelled, fell backward off the horse, and then everything went black.

Farris whistled as he drove up the winding road that led to Aspenglow. Once he had given up his craven impulse to escape to LA, he had instantly felt better. He couldn't run away from his problems.

The sun was low in the sky. As always, this trip felt like coming home. But with India in residence, home held a warmth and a glow of contentment that was even more appealing.

That should have bothered him. And it did. On some level. But he was choosing to live in denial at the moment.

As he pulled up in front of the ranch house, his foreman came running from the direction of the barn. "Mr. Farris," he said, out of breath. "The mare, Daisy, got out of the barn, or someone took her out. She came back wearing a saddle but no rider. I didn't tell Ms. Dottie, 'cause I didn't want to worry her."

The alarm on the man's face told Farris that he knew this was an emergency. Farris felt dizzy for a moment. No one would bother that horse. No one but India.

"Did you see her? Did you see India around the barn today?"

"No, sir. But we've been working elsewhere. Is Jerry going to be okay?"

"He's fine." Jerry's wife had been in town and met them at the ER. "How long ago did the horse wander in?"

"It's been twenty minutes. I sent a couple of guys out to look."

Farris debated his options. They had about two hours of daylight left, maybe less. As soon as the sun went down, temperatures would plummet. Doing an all-out search in the dark would be almost impossible.

"You were right not to upset my mother," he said gruffly. Since Farris had left a message earlier in the day, neither his mother nor the housekeeper would be expecting him. But eventually, they would begin to wonder about India. "Saddle up Diablo for me. I'll grab riding boots from the barn and a bigger coat."

"I'll put the heavy-duty flashlight in the saddlebag."

Farris swallowed hard. "Add the first-aid kit and a blanket. Plus, some water."

"Yes, sir."

The other man ran off. Farris followed rapidly, finding the gear he needed. He was ready in less than five minutes. Two minutes after that, the foreman appeared with Diablo.

Farris mounted and stared toward the mountains. His expression was grim as he assessed his options. "I grabbed the walkie-talkie in case I hit a dead cell spot. The extra one is on the shelf just inside the door. Keep it with you. I might need help."

"Got it."

Farris took off at a gallop, thinking on the run. India

had a terrible sense of direction. They had often laughed about it. Farris would tease her by saying it was her only flaw. There was no way India would simply wander the open range. Surely, she would have kept the fence line in sight.

It was the only clue he had. But if she *had* gotten lost, Farris would have to search in a grid until he found her.

Riding the fence was something he could do on autopilot. How far would she have come? Why had she left the house at all on such a cold day? Admittedly, the weather wasn't bad, as winter days went, but it sure as hell wasn't balmy.

The whole time, he scanned the ground and small clumps of trees for a glimpse of her. Much of the ranch was rolling open prairie. But if the horse had thrown her, India could be anywhere. Thirty minutes passed. Then an hour.

The ice in the pit of his stomach grew. He couldn't leave her out here in the dark, especially after the bear incident. India would be terrified. She was a city girl at heart, though she had grown to love Wyoming as much as Farris did.

He crossed over the dirt road that bisected the ranch and kept going. Five minutes later, he pulled hard on the reins. "Easy, boy. I see something." The sun had glinted off an unknown object in a clump of tumbleweed.

Diablo was well trained. He wouldn't stray. Farris dismounted and took two long strides. Then he realized what he had spotted. It was a cell phone, one he recognized, smashed beyond use. Perhaps the horse had stepped on it.

As Farris explored, he spotted blood. On a rock. His

vision went blurry. India wasn't here. She must have been ambulatory. Which way would she have gone? Surely not farther along the fence. She would have wanted to return to the house. Riding the perimeter would have taken her too far. The road would have been her best choice…unless she had been disoriented.

Carefully, he scanned the dusty ground. Then he found what he was looking for. Footprints, small ones. Feminine ones.

With his heart jolting in his chest, he sprang back into the saddle and eased the horse into motion. It was painstakingly slow. He followed the trail, bit by bit, knowing if he went too fast, he might miss something.

The next ten minutes were the longest of his life. But then he spotted her. A small, crumpled figure leaning against a tree. At least she was upright.

He pulled the horse to a halt and sprang from the saddle. "India. Oh, India. What have you done to yourself?"

She turned her head, blinking at him owlishly. "You're supposed to be in LA," she said, with a puzzled frown.

"I changed my mind." He crouched beside her, touching her chin gently and tilting her face to catch the light. "Damn it, honey." A nasty gash high on her cheekbone still oozed blood. He wasn't even sure stitches would help. The rock had been sharp and jagged. "Where else are you hurt?"

Her eyelids fluttered shut, and her head lolled backward against the tree trunk. "Everywhere," she muttered. "Do you have whiskey? All the cowboys in old Westerns had whiskey for emergencies."

He grimaced. "No whiskey, Inkie. But I can give you a bottle of water."

"That will do."

He had to help hold it, and even then, some of the liquid dribbled down her chin. Because she didn't seem able to catalog her own injuries, Farris ran his hands up and down her arms and legs. It was no easy feat, given the thick down coat she wore. But all the moving parts seemed intact.

India batted his hands away. "This is neither the time nor the place for fooling around, Mr. Farris Quinn. Keep your sexy hands to yourself." Tears welled in her eyes and rolled down her cheeks. "I don't feel so good," she said.

He cursed inwardly. There was no way for him to know if she had internal injuries. On the other hand, she had walked this far at least.

He brushed her hair from her face. "I'm sorry you're feeling rotten, India. We have to get you back to the house." She was visibly shivering now. He worried that she might go into shock.

Getting her onto the horse was tricky. He was strong, but he didn't think he could mount the horse while holding her. If he walked and led the horse back to the barn, it would take far too long.

"Look at me, Inkie."

"Mmm…" She obeyed his command, but her gaze was hazy.

"If I set you on the horse, do you think you can hold on until I get in the saddle?"

"Sure, sure…" Her eyes were closed, which didn't lend much weight to her blithe agreement.

Farris had no choice. Squatting, he gathered her up in his arms and stood, his knees and back screaming from the awkward move.

India whimpered and cried out when he lifted her.

"What is it?" he asked urgently.

Her cheek rested against his chest. "I'm fine," she muttered. "Landed on my hip when I fell, that's all."

He sent up a wordless prayer. "Hang in there, sweetheart. We'll be back at the house in no time."

With all his strength, he eased her up into the saddle. But he didn't let go. Not yet. He curled her fingers around the saddle horn. "Tight, Inkie. Hold it tight."

As far as he could tell, she was following orders, but at any moment she might pitch forward or to one side or the other. He tucked the toe of his boot in the stirrup and swung up behind her. As soon as his arms slipped around her waist, he breathed a sigh of relief. This, he could handle. But he was afraid to let her go long enough even to radio back to the ranch.

Turning Diablo around, he nudged the stallion with his knees, and soon they were trotting back toward the house. The going was smoother once they were on the dirt road. He couldn't tell if India was awake or asleep or even conscious.

Her body rested against his comfortably. He pressed a kiss to her hair and concentrated on the objective.

At the barn, his foreman took Diablo's reins. Farris hopped down and eased India from the saddle, supporting her weight with an arm around her waist. She was milk pale. The gash on her cheek looked even worse now.

Farris addressed his employee, who was alarmed,

judging from the look on his face. "Tell the men thanks for searching. I really appreciate it."

In the house, Farris scooped India into his arms again. "Mother," he called out, hoping she wasn't in her room.

Dottie came running, more of a rapid shuffle, really. "I thought you were in LA," she said. Then she got a good look at India. "Oh, my goodness. What happened?"

"She took Daisy out for a ride. Something spooked the horse. India was thrown, and Daisy wandered back to the barn." Farris kicked open the partially ajar bedroom door, India's bedroom.

When he threw back the bedcovers, India protested. "No, no, no... The sheets are clean, and I'm so dirty."

"Why does it matter?" he said.

Dottie touched his arm. "Easy, son." She smiled at India. "The duvet can be dry-cleaned. We'll put you on top and get a blanket. Okay, dear?"

India nodded.

Dottie smoothed the covers back in place. When Farris laid India gently on the bed, she winced and exhaled sharply.

Farris frowned. "Mother, help me ease her jeans down her legs. She fell on her hip."

Dottie seemed shocked. "I'm not sure..."

India closed her eyes and sighed. "It's fine. He's seen it all anyway."

When mother and son tackled the dusty denim, eventually pulling the jeans to India's ankles, there was a unison gasp. From India, presumably because the maneuver hurt like hell. From Farris and Dottie, because from below India's waist to halfway down her right leg, the skin was a dozen nasty shades of purple, mulberry and black.

Dottie put a hand to her mouth. "Oh, India. I am dreadfully sorry."

"It's my own fault," India muttered. "Daisy had been so compliant… I wasn't holding the reins tightly. A prairie dog spooked her, and I sailed through the air."

Farris shared a wince with his mother. *Good Lord.* "You see her cheek? She hit her head on a rock, too," he said. "I found the blood before I found India."

India touched his hand, her eyes dark with discomfort. "I'm sorry, Farris. Sorry I scared you."

He didn't respond to that. He couldn't. His entire focus was making sure she was okay. "Do you think you can handle a ride into town? We need to get you checked out."

"Oh, no. Please," India said. "All I want is to get cleaned up and have some dinner. Nothing is broken, I swear. My pride took the worst of the hit."

Dottie frowned. "Your face might need stitches."

"I wondered about that." Farris pursed his lips. "But a butterfly bandage might do the trick. Show us you can move your arms and legs."

India had never been so glad to see anyone as she had when Farris showed up. But now she wanted to be alone. To appease the two people staring at her with varying degrees of concern, she bent each arm and leg. "See? No permanent damage."

Dottie seemed relieved. "But your head and your face, dear? I don't want you to have a nasty scar."

"I'll medicate it. I'll make an appointment for a

follow-up. And keep an eye on it. But I don't think I'm vain enough to let it bother me."

Farris still stood there glaring, his arms folded over his chest. "You'll need help getting cleaned up."

It wasn't a question. Farris was an overbearing male issuing an edict.

India bristled. "I most certainly do not."

He glanced at Dottie. "Mother? Do you mind giving us a few minutes alone?"

Dottie's mouth opened and closed, but she didn't say a word. Her gaze went from Farris to India and back again. She nodded and scooted out of the room.

India groaned inwardly. She was hurting both physically and emotionally, and she wasn't sure she had the fortitude to go up against the man who was her Achilles' heel. Even so, it was up to her to get rid of him.

"I appreciate you finding me, Farris. I really do. But I would prefer a bit of privacy to make myself presentable for dinner."

"I can bring you a tray," he said, his gaze stormy.

"No. I don't want Dottie to worry about me. I'll get a shower and some clean clothes and be almost as good as new."

"We had sex last night, India. Why can't I help you with your shower? I'm afraid you might feel faint. A fall in the bathroom could be far worse than what you've already done to yourself."

He was trying to be reasonable. She could see that. He had softened his tone, and even his stance was less aggressively male, more conciliatory. She could get lost in those blue eyes. But one thing gave her pause. One of many, perhaps.

Farris said *we had sex*, not *we made love*. It was a small point. Yet it wounded India. Even though they had agreed to recreational sex, she kept getting confused about how to respond. Could a woman ever really separate emotion from carnal pleasure?

Maybe some women.

But India had been *married* to Farris. And that union had been happy up until the perplexing end.

"I can shower by myself," she said stubbornly. That might be a lie. The thought of standing up and even walking into the bathroom was daunting, much less summoning the energy to wash off several layers of prairie dust.

Farris sat down on the edge of the bed and touched her arm, stroking lightly from her palm to the inside of her elbow. "You're feeling vulnerable. And you're hurting. What if I keep my clothes on, and you wear your undies in the shower? We can get you cleaned up so quickly you won't even have to worry about it."

His face was completely expressionless. He was trying very hard to win her trust.

"I want to be alone," she insisted. "I've been living on my own for five years. I haven't needed you. I *don't* need you now." She was keeping herself together by the thinnest of threads. All the adrenaline from the accident had winnowed away. She hurt all over. There was no energy left to battle Farris.

"I'm sure you don't," he said. "But humor me, please. Why is this such a big deal, Inkie?" His head was cocked, his teasing smile gentle.

"You were gone when I woke up this morning."

His expression closed. He stood up and paced. "You

knew I had ranch work to tend to… My men were waiting to see me."

"You couldn't slow down long enough for breakfast?"

"I wasn't hungry."

His stonewalling made her angry. "You told me you were going to LA *next week*. Then, suddenly, I have to hear from the housekeeper that you're leaving today."

He shrugged. "My plans were fluid."

"And now?"

"I told you. I changed my mind."

"I see."

Her cheek throbbed. Her hip ached. Her whole body was a mess.

There was little doubt left that Farris owed her some answers. It seemed he literally had been trying to run away from her. Was that because she had seen him at his lowest? Those questions and more would have to be postponed until she was more herself.

"Fine," she said, her fingers clenching the sheet. "If it will make you feel better, you can help me."

His face lightened. "Good. That's my girl. Do you want me to carry you in there?"

"No, thank you," she said politely. "I can walk."

She scooted to the edge of the bed and sat up, trying not to cuss. Farris had the good sense not to say a word.

When she began to stand, he put an arm around her waist and helped.

By the time they made it to the bathroom, her forehead was clammy, and she felt weak and light-headed. Without asking, he undressed her down to her bra and panties. "Sit on the stool," he said.

While she leaned against the counter, wishing she had already asked for painkillers, Farris removed his leather belt and kicked off his socks and shoes. She knew she was being ridiculous. But a woman who had been nearly eaten by a bear, deserted by her lover and then thrown from a horse deserved a few eccentricities.

She watched as he turned on the water in the lavish shower stall and adjusted the temperature. He shot her a glance over his shoulder. "You ready?"

She nodded. "Let's get this over with."

"We'll take the stool with us."

India frowned. It was beautiful—handmade—a wrought-iron piece with a woven seat covering. "It will be ruined."

Anger flared in his eyes. "Do you think I care?"

Why was he angry? Was he really so worried about her? Or was it his aborted trip that had him grouchy and short-tempered?

Well, fine. If he wanted to ruin the damn stool, let him.

In the shower, she started to giggle. It was more hysteria than amusement. Farris's eyes widened. "What's so funny?"

She waved a hand. "You. With your clothes all wet. You look ridiculous."

The words were a bald-faced lie. The man was gorgeous on an ordinary day. Now, with his shirt plastered to his body and his hard, muscular frame showcased, he was any woman's fantasy.

India wished he belonged to her.

True to his word, Farris washed her from the top

of her head to her toes without any fanfare. His touch was impersonal.

Her pride was in tatters. Of course, there was no way India could have handled this on her own. And, oh, how wonderful it felt to be clean.

At the very end, Farris removed her bra and wrapped her in a huge towel. Then he steadied her as she stepped out of her wet underwear.

"Do you want to pick out your own clothes?" he asked.

The man was practically supporting her entire weight. Even so, she nodded. "I'll get dressed while you change for dinner."

"If that's what you want." He put her in a chair in the bedroom. "If you get dizzy at all, sit down immediately. I won't be long."

India nodded, and then he was gone. Only because she didn't want him to come back and find her still naked was she able to coax herself into standing. She grabbed a soft bra and panties from a drawer. Putting them on was not easy, but she managed.

In the closet, she found a clean pair of navy sweats that were easy to step into, and then she added a red cashmere sweater. She was hoping the color might cheer her up.

She'd had a glimpse of her bloody cheek already while in the bathroom. It was bad today. Tomorrow it would be worse. In the shower, when Farris had washed her face so gently, the wound had stung like the devil.

When the bedroom door opened, she had just finished adding the tiniest bit of makeup. Anything to make her look perkier than she was.

Seeing Farris caused her heart to skip a beat. He had changed into jeans that were so soft and faded she wondered if he had owned them since college. The fabric molded to his long legs and flat abdomen as if the pants had been made for him.

His feet were no longer bare. Instead, he wore navy wool socks, but no shoes. The navy-and-cream-striped Henley shirt stretched across wide shoulders.

He gave her a searching glance. "You sure you don't want a dinner tray in here?"

She shook her head. "I'm fine."

It would have been personally satisfying to walk from the bedroom to the dining room all on her own. Nevertheless, she might be stubborn, but she wasn't stupid. Fortunately, Farris didn't make a big deal about it. Even when she was forced to lean heavily on his arm, he didn't speak.

Dottie, on the other hand, talked enough for all three of them when they finally sat down to eat. The traditional meal of steak and baked potatoes was augmented with a beautiful green salad. The conversation flowed around India as she concentrated on sitting upright.

It was only when they were having dessert and coffee that her heart began to pound at Farris's words. "Ladies," he said, his smile guileless. "I have news."

Twelve

Farris was under no illusions about India's physical state. The stubborn woman was barely able to hold herself upright.

When he had their attention, he went on, carefully parceling out the speech he had rehearsed. "I don't know if either of you have seen a weather prediction, but we have a monster winter storm on the way. I know the season has been mild so far, but with this system, they're predicting the snow will be measured in feet, not inches."

Dottie grimaced. "That sounds foreboding."

"Exactly," Farris said. "I don't feel comfortable being cut off from civilization, not with your health issues, Mother. I propose we all three fly back to New York tomorrow. To get ahead of the storm. And so India can get checked out by her regular doctor."

It was impossible to gauge India's reaction. Her gaze was on her plate.

Dottie fretted. "Are you sure this is necessary?"

"I am, Mother. But there's more. India?" He waited until he had her attention. "You'll remember, I'm sure, that my mother has volunteered at Saint Mary's Hospital for more than two decades. The hospital guild is having a dinner in less than a week."

India looked at him curiously. "Oh?"

"My mother is being honored with a special award for her years of service. They've been trying to get in touch with her, but you know how she hates email."

Dottie put her hands to her cheeks. "You can't be serious."

He smiled. "Entirely serious. And Herman has asked me if he might escort you."

Dottie blushed. "But he's my—"

Farris held up his hand. "Herman has terminated your professional relationship. He's passed your case files to a colleague. He is very eager to see you, Mom."

India smiled broadly, despite her obvious discomfort. "That's wonderful, Dottie. I'm so happy you're going to be recognized for all your hard work, not to mention having your Herman there. But why didn't they just call you?"

Farris fielded that one. "Mom lost her phone on the trip out here. We never found it. For security reasons, I decided to get her a new number. She's been communicating with friends, but I suppose she forgot to give the hospital her new digits."

Dottie bounced to her feet, her expression agitated. "I should go pack right this instant. Will you need a hand with your things, India?"

Farris gave India a pointed stare. "I can help with that. I've already reserved our flights. We leave at three tomorrow afternoon."

When his mother departed, the room fell silent.

India finished her coffee. "Under the circumstances, I think I'll have an early night. I can throw things in my bags tomorrow morning."

She stood, all the while studiously avoiding his gaze. "Thanks for all your help, Farris. Good night."

The pointed dismissal made him angry, but he kept his temper under wraps. "I'll help you to your room."

She shook her head. "No need. I think I was overly hungry and probably dehydrated. I feel much better now."

"And will we be sleeping together?"

He threw the question at her, watching closely to see how she would respond.

India flinched. He saw her reaction, and it stung.

"I don't think I'm up for sex tonight," she said.

He scowled at her. "Do you really think I'm such an ass? Of course you're not. But I could hold you while you sleep. And I think I should be there in case you need anything. During the night."

India was leaning, using the door frame for support, and she was pale again. His chest ached with love for her. Bringing her to Wyoming had been a good idea on Dottie's behalf, but a terrible situation for Farris.

She was so close and yet so very far away. Nothing he could do could *undo* the past. His body betrayed him time and again, making him yearn for her, burn for her. She was so brave and strong and beautiful. But she wasn't his. Not anymore.

"I'm not sure I want you being nice to me," she said bluntly. Two spots of color burned on her cheekbones. "I'm angry with you."

"Because I didn't see you this morning?" He frowned.

"It's more than that, and you know it. You're interested in sharing my bed, but you won't tell me why you ended our marriage. There's something you're hiding, Farris. I'm not stupid. I've spent five years wondering what it is. And now—I'm over it. Either you tell me what happened, or you and Dottie are on your own when we get to New York."

"You're going to abandon her?"

"If you'll recall, the reason you asked for my help was because you didn't want Dottie to be alone out here at the ranch. You had work to do, and you thought she needed to have company. But those reasons don't apply when we get back to New York. So, what's your choice going to be? You can tell me the truth, Farris, truly. It can't be any worse than what I've imagined."

He ground his jaw. That was where India was wrong. "You're not in any shape for a heart-to-heart. Not tonight."

"And yet tomorrow or the next day your excuse will be something else." She was furious. And she was assertive, confident, strong. The young woman he had once known was gone. Her expression said she wouldn't be cajoled or manipulated.

Everything about this new India aroused him. But

he knew he was doomed to a sleepless, celibate night. "Now is not the time. We need to get you into bed."

"It's barely eight o'clock."

"You're dead on your feet, Inkie. I'll grab you something for pain, something that will help you sleep."

"I don't want to be groggy."

"You won't. But tomorrow is going to be a long day. You need to rest."

It was as if her spirit and her objections collapsed all at once. She seemed so frail suddenly. In that split second, he allowed himself to think about what *might* have happened today. India could have broken her neck. She could be dead.

And Farris would have lost his mind.

In one terrifying moment, he realized that even without anything left of their marriage, he needed to know India was alive. That she was happy and flourishing. Even if her path was not his. Even if he never kissed her or touched her again.

"Come on," he said gruffly, feeling off-balance and uncomfortably emotional. She had always done that to him. She had always undermined his stern stoicism.

Fortunately, India accepted his help. With his arm around her waist, they made the short trip to the blue guest room.

"Do you think you can change clothes on your own?" he asked. "You don't look so great."

Finally, her smile seemed genuine. "Believe me, I know. There's a mirror in the bathroom."

He tucked her hair behind her ear, brushing his lips against her painful-looking wound. "You're as beautiful as always, Inkie. Spending the night in your bed will be torture, but please don't send me away."

She blinked in shock. Perhaps she hadn't expected him to be so open about his lust for her. "Um…"

Before she could divine his intent, he kissed her softly. "You scared the hell out of me today. Don't ever do that again. I don't think my heart can take it."

She rested her cheek against his shoulder. "It scared me, too. I guess I was out cold for a few seconds. No more than that, I think. But Daisy was nowhere in sight."

"She'll be lucky if I don't send her to the glue factory."

"Don't even joke about that. Poor Daisy is a sweetheart. It's not her fault."

"I need *somebody* to blame."

"That would be you," India said tartly, stepping back to glare at him. "I was upset that you took off for California without telling me. That's why I was out riding. I was trying to decide what to do about you."

Grief hit him hard. He had ruined so much. And for what? "There's nothing you can do, India. I shouldn't have asked you to come. I'm sorry."

India was shocked. Farris looked genuinely miserable. For once, he wasn't hiding behind his tough-guy facade. She shrugged. "Well, I'm here for the moment. Why don't you go get ready for bed and come back? I guess we could watch a movie or something."

He stared at her for the longest time, his gaze narrow, as if trying to read her mind. "Or something?"

She felt her cheeks get hot. "Behave, Mr. Quinn. This is a take-it-or-leave-it invitation with an expiration."

He held up both hands. "Got it. But, India?"

"Yes?"

"Please be careful getting ready for bed. If you feel dizzy or faint, sit down immediately."

"I will."

When he was gone, she exhaled. It was hard to be injured and still keep up her defenses against Farris. Letting him spend the night was one more example of her weakness where he was concerned. This setup was a little too cozy. To a stranger, they would look like husband and wife.

India had to keep reminding herself that they weren't.

It took her longer than it should to change into pajamas, but she brushed her teeth and was in bed leaning against the headboard before Farris returned. Even though her body ached all over, seeing her ex-husband striding across the room toward the bed made her heart do a funny little flip.

And her insides buzzed.

Why did he have to be so gorgeous and sexy and appealing? His grin was better than any drug. When he smiled at her like that, she had hope.

"I brought stuff for your face," he said. "You probably should leave it uncovered as much as you can during the day, but I know you don't want to get blood on your pillow." When he sat down on the edge of the bed, she resisted the urge to put distance between them.

"Thank you."

He was silent as he uncapped the antibiotic ointment, spread a small amount on the cut and then layered it with a flexible fabric bandage. The spot where the rock had ripped up her cheek was an awkward one. But the covering he had chosen would move with her face to some extent.

When he was done, he went into her bathroom and washed his hands.

Despite the fact that they had so recently been intimate, India felt her cheeks burn with embarrassment when he returned and climbed into her bed. Planning to have sex was one thing. *Sleeping together* when they weren't a couple felt odd and wrong.

He handed her a bottle of water and a couple of pills that he had put on the nightstand earlier. "Take these," he said.

She didn't bother to argue. Her head and her hip were killing her.

Farris fluffed pillows and made a nest. "Come here, Inkie. Let me hold you."

He was naked from the waist up. In fact, the only thing he wore was a pair of navy knit sleep pants. Underneath those, he was nude. India knew this for two reasons. One, it would never occur to Farris that he *needed* underwear with his jammies. And two, she could see the outline of his erection.

It didn't mean anything. Most men would respond the same when going to bed with a woman, a lover. It was a reflex action. No reason to be flattered.

Torn between reluctance and yearning, she scooted over, wincing and groaning when her body protested. Farris pulled her into his chest and curled an arm around her shoulder, petting it. "I'm sorry you're hurting."

She sighed, her good cheek smashed against a mile of hot male skin. "It's not so bad if I don't move."

He rested his chin on top of her head. "Were you serious about the movie?"

"If you can find anything good to watch, sure."

Farris picked up the remote and aimed it at the TV. India inhaled slowly, breathing in the scent of his shower soap and the male smell that was simply *him*. Surely, after the day she'd had, it wasn't so wrong to drift. To enjoy the moment.

All the problems and realities were still there. Farris had ended their marriage…lied to her by omission. Kept some huge, awful secret. And, honestly, even though she still loved him, the reverse wasn't true.

No man who truly loved a woman would shut her out and send her away.

She must have dozed at some point. When she surfaced the next time, sitting up and eyeing him warily, Farris was halfway through a superhero movie.

He brushed the hair from her sweaty cheek. "How do you feel?" he asked, his voice low and rumbly.

"I'm okay." The medication had done its work. The pain was dulled. "Why do you have the sound muted?"

"I didn't want to disturb you."

They were so close together she could see his individual eyelashes. The ring of deep azure around his pupils sparkled with tiny flecks of amber. His chest rose and fell. "I'll turn out the lights. It's after ten."

All her wants and needs coalesced into one giant knot of despair. As soon as they got back to New York, she wouldn't see Farris again. "Kiss me," she whispered, trying not to cry and ruin the moment. Or betray her utter weakness where he was concerned. She couldn't have him feeling sorry for her. That would be the worst humiliation.

She saw concern in his gaze, but after a moment's hesitation, he eased her down onto her back and leaned over her. "My poor Inkie," he said. The moment his lips touched hers, she shivered and moaned. There was no doubt Farris heard her response.

The kiss deepened. Despite her considerable physical distress, arousal pooled in all the secret places of her body. His lips were firm and warm, coaxing. There was no need for persuasion. She wanted him desperately. This might be the last time.

Farris was more in control than she was. Though the kiss lingered—heated and thorough—he ended it after a few minutes.

It helped that he was visibly shaken. She wasn't alone in this.

"We can't, India," he said, cupping her uninjured cheek with his hand. "There's no way I could keep from hurting you. I won't do that."

She searched his face as he leaned over her. "You did before. You hurt me terribly. And unless I'm mistaken, you're about to do the same thing again."

There was deliberate challenge in her voice. His face went white. Only his eyes burned with *something*. "You should get some sleep," he said, the words perfectly emotionless, even though moments before he'd been kissing her passionately, desperately.

He wasn't going to make love to her. And if she was brutally honest about that euphemism, he wasn't even going to screw her.

She nodded slowly, trying to pretend she wasn't seconds away from begging. "You're right."

Carefully, she rolled onto her left side, facing away from him, wishing she could banish him but knowing she wouldn't.

Farris settled on his side, as well, and spooned her. His big, muscular arms came around her, cradling her in heat and security, though the latter was an illusion.

She felt his lips in her hair. "Good night, India."

"Good night."

She thought she wouldn't sleep. But the exhaustion and the meds did their work. When Farris turned out all the lights and straightened the covers over both of them, she was out in minutes.

It was the best sleep she'd had in five years, despite her poor battered body.

Her dreams were confusing, though. They started out sweet and happy. That was the result of Farris's solid presence and the way his body radiated heat.

But later in the night, her brain ventured into dark territory. She was running. It was one of those dreams where the exits were hidden, and the villain was only steps away.

Sometime around three, she jerked awake, her heart pounding.

Farris roused. "India?" His voice was ragged and sleepy.

"I had a nightmare," she whispered, still facing away from him. It was foolish to admit it, foolish to feel like the dream was a premonition of what was to come.

He nuzzled the back of her neck, running his hand

up and down her arm, trying to comfort her. "I'm here, Inkie. Go back to sleep."

"Okay."

Farris followed his own advice. India lay awake in the dark, her heart breaking. If her entire body didn't ache from being thrown off a horse, she might have tried to seduce him. It would have worked. She and Farris still shared an undeniable, incendiary physical attraction—a connection that defied the truth of their marriage.

His right arm lay curled around her waist. His hand had landed just below her breast. She linked her fingers with his and rubbed one of his big, masculine knuckles with her thumb. Once upon a time, this intimacy, this contentment, had been hers.

How could she let it go again?

But she hadn't let it go the first time, had she?

Instead, she had picked herself up, returned to New York and built the life she wanted. She didn't have a family of her own yet, but it would happen. She was perfectly capable of being happy without Farris. She had reached that point a few years ago. But what if the best version of herself and her life was the one that included Farris?

Not only that, but what if she was the only person who could make *him* happy? What if her leaving had been far more detrimental to him than to her? What if Farris *needed* her?

What if his secrets were slowly destroying him?

"Why?" she whispered in the dark. "Why won't you tell me?"

Maybe she would hire a private investigator. Maybe

she could find out what terrible sin Farris had committed. A woman he had slept with…cheating on his wife? No matter how much she tried to find something big enough, bad enough, to end a marriage, that was the extent of her imagination.

Farris had loved her once. The physical need was still there.

And then it hit her. Even if India hired the damn FBI and they investigated every nook and cranny of Farris's life, even if they discovered the truth, it wouldn't matter. The reason the marriage had ended was because Farris didn't trust her with the truth. As far as she could tell, nothing had changed.

She stared dry-eyed at the ceiling, wishing she didn't have to endure the next day. She wanted to hole up in her apartment and forget this interlude.

Her heart had healed before…mostly. She could do it again…maybe.

For now, she would drink in this moment. It would have to sustain her for a very long time. Trusting someone else eventually—building a new relationship with a stranger, falling in love—those things were possible.

But the truth was a bitch. She didn't want another husband. She wanted Farris…

Thirteen

When Farris woke up the next morning, India was gone. *Damn it.* His arms were empty, and his head throbbed. How had she left without him realizing? He rubbed a hand over his face, trying to ignore his aching erection. It had been that way for most of the night. Holding his ex-wife for eight or nine hours straight had been heaven and hell.

What was she up to now? The bathroom door was open. She wasn't in there.

He rolled out of bed and went to his own room to shower and dress. By the time he made it to the dining room, the smell of food was tempting, but his mood was somewhere between rabid coyote and wounded grizzly bear.

Because his mother was at the table, he managed a smile. "Good morning, Mom. How did you sleep?"

Dottie eyed him with an odd expression. "Better than you, I think. You look terrible, Farris."

"Gee, thanks." He sat down and loaded his plate with eggs and sausage and homemade applesauce. "Where's India?" he asked. "Did she eat already?"

"I assume she's still in her room. We shouldn't bother her until we have to… She probably feels dreadful this morning, poor thing."

Farris felt his stomach curl as nausea flooded his system. Surely, India wouldn't have walked out on him. She'd been pissed. That was true. And she had laid her cards on the table, so there was no mystery. But she didn't have a car. Still, all she had to do was pluck the keys from the hook by the back door.

He cleared his plate on autopilot. He was pretty sure Dottie talked to him. Maybe he answered.

Finally, he sprang to his feet. "I have to check on a few things before we leave. Are you all packed?"

Dottie beamed. "Sure am. I'm excited, Farris. I've loved being here in Wyoming with you and India, but I'm ready to go home to New York."

"Me, too, Mom," he said. The lie threatened to stick in his throat. "I'll see you in a little while."

He strode out of the room and down the hall, bellowing as he neared his room and India's. "Inkie! Where in the hell are you?" Flinging open her door, he sucked in a sharp breath as he nearly knocked her down.

She was completely dressed, with her blond hair shiny and clean. Her hazel eyes were more green than brown this morning. The minimal makeup she wore accentuated her pallor. Black wool pants and an expensive teal sweater clung to her curves. "I'm right here," she said, her tone mild. "Why all the yelling?"

"Where did you go?"

"I don't understand."

He counted to ten. "When I woke up, you were gone."

Her smile was cool. "Doesn't feel so good, does it? But as much as I'd like to claim that little bit of payback, there was no ulterior motive. I woke up early... couldn't get back to sleep. I've been in the walk-in closet packing my things. I had the door closed, so I wouldn't wake you."

"Oh." Now he felt foolish. But at least his heart settled down. "Do you need help with the packing?"

India yawned. "No, thanks. I stuffed as much as I could in my suitcase and carry-on, but I'll have to get the rest of my things shipped. Do you think your housekeeper would mind going to the post office? I saved the boxes my friend used to send my winter clothes. I've filled the packages and taped them up. They aren't terribly heavy."

"I'm sure she'll be happy to do that for you." He studied her face. "On a scale of one to ten, how are you feeling?"

"So-so." India shrugged. "Sore, stiff. Nothing I can't handle."

She was telling him she didn't need his help, his hovering. He got the message. But though he respected her wishes, he couldn't turn off his own feelings about the matter. Today would be long and tiring. India needed his protection.

"We'll leave for the airport at noon," he said. "Box

lunches in the car. Don't you dare try to carry your bags. Put them in the hall when they're ready, and I'll take care of it."

India stared at him, her expression impassive. "I'll be ready."

He hesitated, torn by decisions he'd made long ago. "India, I..."

She lifted an eyebrow. "Yes?"

For one incredible moment, India thought she had finally gotten through to him. She could almost see the words trembling on his tongue, eager to be spoken. *Tell me, Farris. Tell me.*

Apparently, old habits were hard to break, and old secrets sacred.

His face closed up, and his body language froze her out. "I have to speak to my foreman before we leave," he muttered. "I'll see you at noon."

India swallowed her disappointment. She wasn't surprised. Not at all. Her relationship with Farris was definitely over. Neither wife nor lover would accompany him to New York. From now on, India would protect her heart.

She shoved her hands in her pockets and walked around the room, making sure she had gathered all her personal items. She wouldn't be coming back to Wyoming. Ever.

Even if Dottie passed away here and not in New York, India didn't think she could handle Farris and a funeral. But what if he needed her?

Too bad, she told herself firmly.

At the appointed hour, she climbed into the back seat

of Farris's car and settled in for the trip to the airport. Dottie sat up front, chattering excitedly.

Farris drove with both hands on the wheel, white-knuckled. To India, his mood seemed volatile, but that might have been an illusion. Why would *he* be tense or upset?

At the airport, he sprang the next surprise. "I chartered a small jet," he said. "The storm will be affecting a lot of commercial flights. I didn't want to take a chance of getting stuck somewhere along our itinerary."

Dottie was delighted. "Oh, how fun," she said. "I know it's an indulgence, but it's so much more peaceful. And, India," she said, "this will be infinitely better for you. No jostling in the center aisle. You'll be able to relax."

India smiled and nodded, beyond words. She and Farris had flown private jets once or twice during their brief marriage. Though she had loved being pampered, the cost involved made her slightly ill. Surely, Farris remembered that.

In the small plane, four rows of seats were configured in sets of two, an aisle and a third single. Before anyone could say a word, India commandeered a solo seat, leaving Farris and his mother to sit together. She requested a pillow from the male attendant and settled down to sleep. Her unsettled night had caught up with her. Oblivion beckoned.

Later, she had no idea how long the flight had taken. She'd been comatose most of the way across the country. When she finally sat up and ran her hands through her hair, the lights of New York twinkled below.

Deplaning at LaGuardia was fast and easy. The tall

young man who had worked the flight procured a luggage cart. He spoke to Farris deferentially. "The car will meet you near the taxi stand, sir. I've confirmed your reservation, and I'll make sure the bags are loaded into the trunk."

India gave the young man a smile. "I have my own rideshare coming," she said. "That large blue suitcase and the matching carry-on are mine. I'll get them from you as we exit the terminal, if that's okay?"

When she turned around, both Farris and Dottie stared at her with indignation.

Farris broke the small silence. "Don't be absurd, India. We'll drop you off."

She shook her head firmly. "My apartment is in the complete opposite direction. I appreciate the offer, but this makes more sense."

For the next twenty minutes, she was able to ignore Farris in the hubbub of the airport. An attendant had shown up with a wheelchair for Dottie.

Once they were outside the building, India breathed a sigh of relief. Her escape was almost complete. "Goodbye, Dottie. I had a wonderful time with you in Wyoming. I hope your hospital gala is amazing."

Dottie's eyes shone with tears, but she was calm. "It was wonderful to spend time with you again, India. Let's keep in touch." India hugged Farris's mother.

Then the only hurdle left was bidding her ex-husband goodbye. With her heart breaking, she managed a breezy smile. "This has been so much fun. I wish you all the best, Farris." She went up on her tiptoes and kissed his cheek.

He tried to pull her close for a real kiss, but a wave

of passengers exited the building, and she managed to elude him. "Take care," she called over her shoulder. Then she dashed across the lanes of taxis and buses and jumped into a navy Sentra, wrestling her bags into the car with her.

The driver was a young Hispanic woman. "Where to, ma'am?"

India rattled off her address and sat back, feeling empty.

She gave herself a pep talk. These wretched feelings would pass. As soon as she got home, she would call her boss and smooth over any ruffled feathers, so she could get back to work. She would buy theater tickets and plan a dinner date with a few of her closest friends. Spring wasn't so terribly far away. The earth would awaken from its long winter's sleep. India looked forward to the flowers, the abundant sunshine, the promise of summer.

The Farris Quinn chapter was over. Now she could get back to her normal, enjoyable life.

Nothing had really changed. She was single and living in one of the world's most fascinating cities. Everything was going to be good.

Four days after returning from Wyoming, India was a mess. Her very nice apartment had greeted her with stale air and a pervasive feeling of loneliness. India did laundry, and she cried. She took walks in the park and came home to cry. She cooked pasta dinners for one… and cried. The yawning emptiness inside her chest was terrifying. All she could think about was how wonderful it had been to have Farris back in her bed and in her life.

She grieved all over again.

On the fourth morning, she pulled herself together. No more moping. In a few days, she had a meeting with her boss to see if she still had a job. He had stonewalled her at first. On the plus side, she had come back to New York earlier than she had promised.

In the negative column, she had walked out on him with very little notice. Truthfully, she couldn't blame him if he let her go.

Oddly, that thought didn't bother her as much as it should. She definitely would explore her other options after she quit feeling numb.

That afternoon, she decided to take herself out for an early dinner. Being cooped up inside was not helping her mood. She put on the black pants and teal sweater she had worn on the trip back from Wyoming. It was a deliberate choice. She needed to make new memories, even with her favorite clothes. It had rained earlier, but the rain had stopped, leaving the air misty and cool. She chose low-heeled pumps and decided to walk to the restaurant. Her black raincoat was lined. It would keep her warm enough. She picked up her purse and her keys, ready to depart, but the doorbell rang.

The young couple in the apartment across the hall ordered takeout frequently. Delivery people who didn't pay attention often ended up at India's door. But just in case—because she was security conscious—she put her eye to the peephole to see who it was.

The man standing on the other side of her door was definitely not a delivery person. He had his hands shoved in his pockets. His expensive overcoat made him look like he had stepped out of the pages of a magazine.

Her heart bounced in joy and then dropped to her

shoes. Why had Farris come? Why now when she had forced herself to think positively, to take her eyes off the past and look toward the future?

The doorbell rang a second time. She could almost hear Farris's impatience.

With a preternatural sense of calm, she opened the door. "Farris. What are you doing here?"

Fourteen

Farris was in hell. He couldn't sleep. He couldn't eat. He was so screwed. Because what he had done in the past couldn't be undone.

Seeing India framed in the doorway was shocking in a way he couldn't explain. Both wonderful and terrible. He'd tried to convince himself that their intimacy in Wyoming had been nothing more than a case of convenience.

A sexual auld lang syne…

Now, seeing her in the flesh, he understood the magnitude of what he had lost. Again…

"Hello," he said quietly, waiting for her to invite him in. He'd never actually been inside India's apartment. She had rented it after the divorce.

She jingled the keys in her hand. "I was on my way out," she said.

Only when she said the words did he see that she was wearing a coat. "This won't take long," he said.

She lifted an eyebrow. "I'll ask you again, Farris. Why are you here?"

He skipped the persuasive buildup he had planned and forged ahead. "Dottie wants you to be at the gala. In fact, she's insisting on it. She wants you to meet Herman. She wants you to see her get the award." He shifted from one foot to the other. "You'd be my plus-one."

The only indication that India had heard and processed his torrent of words was the way her beautiful eyes widened. "No," she said simply.

It was painfully clear to him that he was pleading the case, not primarily for his mother's benefit, but for his own. And he wasn't above playing dirty pool. "You can't disappoint her," he said. "This night, this award, her new beau—all of these may be the highlights of her adult life. We don't know how much time she has left."

India stared at him. "Emotional blackmail? Really, Farris? That's pretty low, even for you."

"Please," he said, willing her to give in. "It's just one night." He touched her face gently. "Your cheek is looking much better."

Seconds ticked by, then an entire minute. Her shoulders rose and fell. "Fine," she said. "Give me the address, and I'll meet you there. I assume it's black-tie?"

He nodded. "It is. But I'll pick you up. I have a driver. We'll swing by around five thirty. Mother wants us all to have a drink at the hotel bar before we head into the ballroom for the dinner and the main event."

"I said I'll meet you there."

He reached for her hand, but she jerked it back. "Please, India," he muttered. "Don't punish Dottie for my sins."

At one time, India's hazel eyes had looked at him with love and adoration. He missed those days desperately. He missed the couple they had been, he and this warm, generous, sexy woman.

India's expression chilled. Her gaze was icy. "This is the last time, Farris. I won't let you manipulate me anymore. One night. For Dottie's sake. After that, I don't ever want to see you again." She stepped back and shut the door in his face.

Farris walked for miles after that. Cabs were plentiful in this neighborhood, but he needed the cold air to clear his head.

He needed to think.

For the first time, he let himself imagine telling India the truth. She claimed he could tell her anything. Did she still love him? He suspected she might. Why else would she have shared his bed...and hers?

As one block bled into another, he walked. Head down, chest tight. Without conscious thought, he traced a route that took him in front of the restaurant where he had proposed to India. She had been so young, so beautiful, so trusting. He had promised himself that night that he would spend the rest of his life cherishing her.

But in no time at all, he had let a driving need for revenge destroy the most perfect love he had ever known. He'd held the keys to happiness in his hands, but he had tossed them in the murky river of his own deceit and self-loathing.

He paced the floors of his spacious apartment that night as he struggled with the urge to bare his soul, to tell her everything. At one time, he had been that romantic cliché—the knight in shining armor. India's love had polished and perfected him.

But he had been greedy. He hadn't wanted to give up his past mistress. He hadn't wanted to give up the old vendetta.

So he had lost his wife.

By the time his driver pulled up in front of India's building the following evening, Farris had worked himself into a state of turmoil. He entered the elevator in the lobby, pushed a button and stared at his reflection in the polished brass.

The elevator stopped. Farris got out. He walked to India's door with his heart beating in his throat.

He knocked. Moments later, the door swung open. India stood there, her slender, enticing curves emphasized in sin-red silk. The dress hugged her body like a lover. The low-cut bodice was supported by the tiniest of spaghetti straps. A man could snap either one with a single hand.

"You look amazing." He swallowed hard, envisioning an endless evening of wanting what he could not have. Her arms and shoulders were bare. A diamond pendant nestled just at the top of her cleavage. Matching earrings dangled from her small, delicate earlobes.

"Thank you," she said. "I know it's winter, but hotel ballrooms are always hot. I won't be the only woman there to choose *glam* over gloomy. Winter needs spicing up. A fancy party, a new dress. I'm ready to go."

She reached for her faux fur wrap. It was a cape-like

affair with a single rhinestone clasp at the front. Farris took it from her and tucked it around her shoulders, careful not to muss her hair.

"I'll be the envy of every man there," he said lightly, trying to pretend that she wasn't destroying him bit by bit.

They didn't speak in the car. Each of them sat in a corner of the back seat with a large no-man's-land in between.

What was she thinking?

The hotel was awash in tuxedo-clad men and brightly plumaged women. In the bar, Dottie greeted India with a hug. "You look absolutely riveting, sweet girl. I want you to meet Herman."

Farris watched from a mental distance as the other three conversed. He inserted a response when necessary, but he was content to sip his Scotch and study India when she didn't know he was watching her.

His ex-wife's laugh lit up the room. Herman was charmed. Dottie was delighted. Only Farris would be a loser tonight.

When they finally abandoned the cozy, dimly lit bar, checked their coats and made their way into the ballroom, Dottie grew silent. Herman had her hand in his, but Dottie was clearly abashed by the upcoming attention.

Farris kissed his mother's cheek. "Relax, Mother. Everyone here thinks you're the best. This is your night."

As they took their seats, India put her napkin in her lap and glanced at him with an odd expression. "That was one reason I fell for you in the beginning," she said quietly. "I loved the way you cared for your mother. I decided that any man with so much honor and respect for the woman who birthed him was a man who would never let me down."

"Inkie," he groaned. Her words tore him apart.

But the evening's festivities were well underway.

The meal was served seamlessly. Farris barely tasted anything he ate. India seemed to enjoy the food. As did everyone else at the table.

Then came the champagne and the awards. A few hospital staff were recognized. A donor who was funding a new cancer treatment center. And finally, it was time for the volunteers.

The emcee handed out a few five-year recognitions. A couple of ten-year. Then it was Dottie's moment. The chief administrator stood at the podium and spoke eloquently about Dottie's cheerful, steadfast service to the public during her many years at Saint Mary's.

Herman beamed. The distinguished man took Dottie's arm and escorted her to the stage. As the room clapped and cheered, Dottie stepped to the microphone. It had to be lowered for her.

"I am so honored," she said, her voice quavering with emotion. "The truth is, volunteering is selfish, really. I find great reward in getting to know the patients and staff at Saint Mary's. Like many people, I suffered through hard times early in my life. But that is far in the past. What I want to do now, what I've always wanted to do, is to live each day with purpose and joy." She looked out across the room. "The one person I need to thank more than any other is my son, Farris Quinn. He has been my rock and my protector since he was very young."

She blew a kiss to Farris, who managed a smile.

Then Dottie went on. "I appreciate this recognition more than you know. It reminds me that we are all connected, we are all family. If any of you have considered volunteering at Saint Mary's, I encourage you to jump right in. It's never too late to do the right thing."

Farris felt his face burn. Was that a dig at him? Or were Dottie's words a coincidence? There was no way she could know what he had done.

When his mother returned to the table, her mood was bubbly.

Farris stood and kissed her cheek. "Thank you, Mother. That was a sweet speech."

Herman nodded. "Beautifully done, Dottie."

"You were eloquent," India said.

At that moment, the emcee wrapped things up and urged the crowd to adjourn to the adjacent ballroom where an orchestra was already playing.

Herman lifted Dottie's hand and kissed it. "I'd like to dance with the star of the evening."

"Oh, pooh," Dottie said. "I was one of many." But her bashful, pleased smile said she appreciated being the center of attention.

In three minutes, eight people departed the table. Only Farris and India were left.

His date stared at her phone, shutting him out.

"It will look odd if we don't dance," he said.

Her head shot up. Her expression was impenetrable. "I'm going to grab a cab."

"Are you scared of me, Inkie?" The words came out sounding like a challenge. He hadn't even known he was going to say them.

Anger flashed in her eyes. "Don't be absurd. Besides, I fulfilled my duty. Drinks at the bar, dinner, awards. What more do you want from me?"

Everything. He needed to loosen his bow tie. The room was overly warm, as India had predicted. After taking a swig from his water glass, he stood. "You told me that tonight is it. You never want to see me again. So I might as well get my money's worth from this date. My mother will be hurt if you leave without saying goodbye. It's just dancing."

India's gaze narrowed. Her tight-lipped expression said she was angry. But she didn't make a scene. Although she wouldn't take his hand, she also stood and preceded him into the ballroom. Farris took her tiny black satin clutch and tucked it in his jacket pocket.

"Shall we dance?" he asked. His voice was hoarse, and his hands trembled.

He took India in his arms. They had danced many times before during their marriage. Perhaps it was like riding a horse…or muscle memory. Stepping into the flow of the music and the swirl of the crowd was effortless.

Her skin was warm and smooth beneath his fingertips where his hand rested on her back. He held her circumspectly, but even so, his body responded. It had been days since he had made love to her, days that felt like an eternity.

Dottie's innocent words echoed in his brain. *It's never too late to do the right thing.*

Every time he thought about telling India the truth, his courage failed him.

The music went on forever, from one dance to the

next. India's cheek rested against his lapel now. A strand of her hair tickled his nose.

As long as the band kept playing, everything was perfect.

But not all fairy tales had happy endings.

Dottie and Herman appeared from the midst of the crowd. Dottie looked exhausted but happy. She hugged India and then her son. "I'm so glad you both were here tonight. I'm very tired. Herman has offered to take me home."

Herman's hand rested protectively in the small of Dottie's back. Farris liked and respected the man, but given Dottie's diagnosis, he didn't know if it was a good idea for his mother to get involved.

"I'm happy to take you, Mother," he said.

Dottie shook her head. "I've invited Herman to have a cup of decaf with me and catch up on all the gossip in our corner of New York. Before tonight, we haven't seen each other in three months." The smile she gave the older man was soft and sweet.

Farris had no option but to smile, as well. "You two kids be careful going home."

When the goodbyes were over and the other couple exited the room, India looked at him. "May I have my purse, please? I'm going to catch a cab and call it a night."

There was absolutely no expression on her face at all.

In that instant, Farris realized the truth. If he let her walk away this time, it was over. Beyond over.

He cleared his throat. "I was hoping we could talk."

One of her eyebrows went up. She glanced at her

watch. "Now? It's late, Farris." There was impatience in her voice and a clear desire to escape.

"It's important." His throat was so tight he was barely able to squeeze the words out. When he looked at her, his heart ripped in half, possibly a fatal wound. With everything inside him, he willed her to say yes.

She rubbed two fingers against the center of her forehead as if she might have a headache. "This isn't exactly an opportune moment, in case you haven't noticed. There are a million people in this hotel, and it's too cold to walk outside."

He inhaled sharply. India was opening the door for a possible conversation. She had assessed what *wouldn't* work. It was up to him to find a solution. "We can go back to my place."

She flinched. "No."

His brain raced. "I could get us a room here," he said. "No funny business. Just a quiet spot where we might take our shoes off and relax. I give you my word. All I want is a chance to explain."

Suddenly, she paled. He saw suffering in her eyes. "Explain what?"

Here it was. The all-or-nothing roll of the dice. His body went numb. "Explain what happened to our marriage."

India swayed, gray-faced now. Haunted. He actually thought she might faint.

He took her arm and steered her through the dancers. The band was still playing, but he couldn't hear the music, because his ears were buzzing or ringing or *something*.

The hallway was marginally less crowded than the ballroom.

"India?"

Her nod was almost imperceptible. "Okay."

They retrieved their coats. Moments later in the lobby, he thought about finding her a chair while he checked in. But he was afraid she might bolt. So he kept her with him.

When he approached a uniformed clerk and requested a room, the man offered two choices. Farris picked the suite with a sitting area. That way there would be no bed to look at. No temptation to get sidelined by sex. He scrawled his name on the reservation form. Then he curled his arm around India's waist and escorted her to the bank of elevators. When they entered, other guests joined them.

India focused her gaze on the polished floor.

Farris watched the numbers light up on the panel. At each floor, people got off. By the time the elevator reached the top, Farris and India were the only ones left.

He didn't touch her as they walked down the hall. Their suite was on the corner with panoramic vistas, or so he'd been promised. Once he dealt with the key card and opened the door, they entered to find a luxurious set of rooms decorated in beautiful but very traditional furnishings.

The plush carpet and jewel-tone colors were inviting on a cold winter night.

India immediately commandeered a comfy armchair. She kicked off her high heels and curled up with an audible sigh.

Farris was momentarily stymied. The script eluded him. "Would you like anything to drink?" he asked. "We have a minifridge. Or room service."

"No, thanks." India chewed her bottom lip.

To postpone the inevitable, he went to the window and opened the heavy drapes. The lights of New York spread out in every direction. "Nice view," he said, wincing at the inane sound of his own voice.

"Say what you have to say, Farris."

He whirled around to face her. The subtext was clear. India wanted to leave.

"Okay." He loosened his bow tie and tossed it aside. Then he discarded his jacket and rolled up his shirt-sleeves. His shoes were next. At last, he made himself face her, even though it was like looking at the sun. She dazzled him. He cleared his throat. "Do you still love me, India?"

Her mouth gaped. Temper flashed in her eyes. "Go to hell."

He hoped she did love him. He thought she might—in spite of everything—but he couldn't be sure. If she *didn't*, this explanation probably made no difference anymore. Except that maybe India would see that the breakup of their marriage had nothing to do with her. Farris shouldered all the blame.

He sat down on the sofa and leaned forward with his elbows on his knees. Studying the intricate design in the carpet was far easier than looking her in the eye.

Finally, he jumped in. "From about the time I turned sixteen, I made it a point to know everything there was to know about Edward Simpson's life, his real family, his business interests. I was obsessed with my hatred of him. Although it made no sense, especially as a teenager, I swore to myself that I would even the score one day."

India spoke, her tone low and without nuance. "Your mother told me she took you to counseling."

He sat back and shrugged, finally managing to meet her gaze. "Even the best shrink needs more than six months to eradicate the kind of anger I nursed. It was a millstone around my neck, but I carried it proudly, even if I was the only one who knew the extent of those feelings."

India's smile was bleak. "Didn't you ever hear that old saying…revenge is like drinking poison and expecting the other person to die?"

Farris winced. "Possibly."

"But what does this have to do with me? You never even talked to me about your father, except in the most tangential ways."

"I'm getting to that." How did he explain the black hole that had consumed him? "Everything was fine in the beginning. You and I were newlyweds."

Now her expression was wry. "I know. I was there."

"I barely even thought about him. I was happy, India, so happy. And that was all you. Even the business consumed less of my attention. For the first time in my life, I was looking ahead and not to the past."

"But somewhere along the line that changed," India said. "I don't think we even made it two years, did we? That's when you started to pull away from me."

Thinking about those days and weeks brought him deep shame. He was a highly educated, supposedly intelligent man. He'd had a young, beautiful wife whom he adored. A challenging career. But it hadn't been enough.

"I was like an addict in a way," he said slowly. "I'd

been *clean* for months, and then something happened that pulled me back into the pit. I'm sorry, India. You'll never know how sorry. I regret everything I did to us. I was ashamed. I knew I had done something that you would hate, and I hated myself. The chasm grew so wide I couldn't find my way across."

Fifteen

India was cold, so cold, and it wasn't the temperature in the room. She was chilled with fear. There had been many times over the last five years when she had wondered if she really wanted to know the truth. Now the moment was at hand, and she wasn't sure she could bear the revelations she was about to hear.

Farris looked like a man being tortured, stretched on a rack, made to walk over fiery coals. She would have stopped him if she could. But she had begged for this moment, demanded it. Now she couldn't escape the consequences.

Instead, she stood and grabbed his tuxedo jacket off the chair where he had tossed it. She slipped her arms into the sleeves and burrowed into the protection it provided. Any lingering warmth from his body had dissipated, but the coat carried his scent.

"I was wrong," she said quietly. "You don't owe me any explanations. Not after all this time. You and I have both moved on. Whatever it is, I forgive you, I swear."

He paced the floor now, as if sitting still was more than he could handle. "It's time," he said. "Time for you to know the truth."

"Okay." She braced herself, unable to anticipate what was coming. "Go on. What happened?"

He ran both hands through his hair. Even rumpled, he was masculine grace personified. He had carried secrets, but in the early part of their marriage, she had never felt a gulf between them.

She saw the muscles in his throat ripple as he swallowed. "I had a chance to annihilate the man who married my mother illegally and made me a bastard."

"Oh, Farris. What did you do?" Had he really destroyed Simpson and dealt with the guilt ever since?

Farris opened the minibar, found a tiny bottle of Scotch and downed it like a man taking medicine. "A guy came to me, an acquaintance, someone who had no idea who my father was or what had happened to me in the past. This person told me about a hot stock deal. It was going down the following day. But if I wanted in, I had to act fast."

"I don't understand."

"Someone had initiated a hostile takeover of Simpson's business empire. All I had to do was buy a significant number of shares, and I could watch Simpson lose everything. It was what I had waited for all these years."

"But it wasn't your idea. Maybe you were wrong to

buy those shares, but you don't have to feel guilty about that. It was going to happen anyway, right? They would have found someone else to invest."

Farris shook his head slowly. He was pale. Beneath his perpetually golden skin, his color was bad. His eyes burned with emotion. "Don't try to make excuses for me, Inkie. This is only the beginning."

She began to shiver. And she couldn't think of a single thing to say.

He continued to pace. "You may have heard people call me the Ice Man."

"Once or twice."

"I'm known in business as the guy who never plays the market with emotion. I study. I assess. I compute the odds. And I invest based on those principles. But when this opportunity to bury Simpson came along, I jumped at it. My hatred and my vendetta blinded me to everything but a driving desire to punish him."

"I see." She didn't really. She didn't understand anything at all. But she had to say *something*.

Farris continued his story as if he was watching a movie from the past and narrating. Only this was much more visceral.

He lifted his gaze and stared at her with an expression that broke her heart. "I lost everything, India. It was a bad investment."

"Bad, how?"

He muttered something under his breath. "There are a hundred reasons why, but the short answer is that I let down my guard, and I sold my cow for some magic beans. I lost ten million dollars, India. Overnight."

She blinked, not sure she had heard him correctly. "Ten mil—"

He held up a hand, cutting her off. "You heard me. I was panic-stricken. All I could think about was how your father had gambled away your family home and left you an orphan. On our wedding day, I had promised to love and cherish you in sickness and in health, but at the first opportunity, I betrayed your trust in me."

Now it was her turn to pace. The carpet was soft beneath her bare feet, but she ached all over. "Why didn't you tell me?"

He leaned against the door, his mouth set in a grim line. "I was embarrassed, humiliated, distraught. I couldn't bear to see the look in your eyes when you realized how badly I had failed you. I had to liquidate almost everything we owned, India. Stocks, bonds, a few properties I had acquired as investments. Somehow, I managed to hold on to the ranch and our apartment. But even that was dicey."

"I can't believe this."

She began to look back, to relive those months. In the context of what she had just learned, some of Farris's bizarre behavior began to make sense. No wonder he had been distant. No wonder he had begun sleeping alone.

"I'm so sorry, Farris," she said. Tears dripped down her cheeks. "I should have seen how you were hurting. I should have helped you."

His look was incredulous. "No."

"I heard what you told me. You lost all our money. I get it. And you didn't think I was strong enough or smart enough to walk beside you."

"That's not what I meant."

She shrugged. "Sounds like it to me."

"My God, I hated myself. You should hate me, too."

"I never did like people telling me what I should and shouldn't do. I'm kind of stubborn that way." She paused, curious suddenly. "So did you claw your way back? Am I looking at a pauper, or a man with plenty of zeros in his checkbook?"

She cocked her head and smiled at him. Suddenly, happiness bloomed in her heart and spread everywhere, warming her, giving her hope.

Farris's jaw dropped. Again, he swallowed. "Does it matter?"

"Actually, no. Not at all."

His brows pulled together in suspicion. "Why not?"

She went to him, no longer able to keep her distance. When she put her hands on his broad, muscular shoulders, she felt the shudder that quaked through his body. "Because I love you," she said simply, searching his beautiful eyes. "From that first moment you ran into me and knocked me down in Central Park, I knew I had found my one and only."

Farris didn't move. His whole body was tensed, like a giant jungle cat sensing danger.

She saw his jaw work before he spoke. "You're not furious?"

"Well…" She sighed. "I'm not happy. You cost us five years when we could have been together, five years we won't ever get back."

"I know." He rested his forehead against hers. "I'm sorry."

Suddenly, she remembered something else, something shocking. "That's why you wouldn't get me pregnant, isn't it? Because you lost all our money?"

"Yes."

She punched him in the arm. Hard. "You're an ass. Good Lord, Farris. We could have had two precious babies by now."

"You're not making me feel better," he said. His smile was not much of a smile, but some of the dark misery had left his eyes.

"I think you've left out one piece of the story."

He was affronted. "I most certainly did not. I've told you everything."

She kissed him briefly, a brush of lips that brought her tears back. Was it really possible? Had they survived the shipwreck that was their marriage?

"Think hard," she said. "I'm starting to get an inferiority complex."

"Oh, that." He chuckled, though the laugh was rusty. "I adore you, Inkie. And I have for every moment of every day. You are the love of my life. Those five years were an eternity for me. And yes, it's absolutely true. I never looked at another woman."

For the first time, she believed him without reservation. "I know."

"I'm sorry I didn't lean on you," he said. "I'm sorry I didn't tell you the truth. I swear I'll never do that to you, to us, again."

They held each other then, hearts beating wildly, emotions careening.

Farris's chest rose and fell as he sucked in a huge breath and exhaled. "My mother will be over the moon."

"I don't want to lose her."

"Me, either. Maybe this news will give her a boost." He kissed her forehead, each of her eyes, the tip of her nose. "So what now?"

"Isn't it obvious, my love? You marry me again, and then you get me pregnant as fast as you can."

He stroked her back, his hands landing on her ass. "Ah," he said. "I like that plan."

India slid her arms around his neck and pressed closer. "How much time do we have?"

"You mean in this room?"

"Yes."

"They don't rent by the hour. It's a fine, upstanding property. We'll need to be out by noon tomorrow."

She began unbuttoning his shirt, drunk with relief and arousal and gratitude. "Is there a bed nearby?"

Farris kissed her wildly and lifted her off the floor. His erection throbbed against her belly. "Through that door," he muttered.

He scooped her into his arms and carried her into the bedroom.

India raised an eyebrow when she saw the rose petals on the duvet. "Good grief, Farris. Is this the—"

A glimmer of his rakish, naughty, bad-boy smile returned. "The honeymoon suite? Yes, ma'am."

"I love a man who's always prepared," she said smugly.

He lowered the zipper on the back of her dress. When he saw the black strapless bra and matching thong, he sucked in a breath. "Holy hell. I don't know which is better—you au naturel under a dress, or this get-up."

"I'm glad you approve." When he started to remove

her undies, she batted his hands away. "My turn to un-wrap you," she said.

"Nope." He ripped off his shirt, pants and boxers in record time.

India sat on the edge of the bed and took in the show. "Oh, my." Some men might look awkward standing there naked except for a pair of dark socks. Not Farris. He dispensed with his last two items of clothing and closed the gap.

"Sorry, love. Couldn't wait. I happen to know you're a tease."

She threw a rose petal at him. "Couldn't wait for what?"

"You." He eased her onto her back and stretched out beside her, his gaze dark with passion and a dozen other emotions. He touched her right hip gently. "You still have a bruise. Poor Inkie."

"It doesn't hurt anymore." She focused her eyes on his face, the classic profile, the kissable lips. She wanted him badly, and she saw the same yearning in his gaze. Maybe they were both afraid this was a dream. She floated on a cloud of contentment laced with urgency and heat. "Besides, it was worth it if that crisis con-vinced you that you couldn't live without me."

Farris sobered, his fingers still stroking her hip. "Don't joke." He bent to kiss the remnants of her clash with the ground. "That was one of the worst days of my life."

She lifted her hips and tugged her panties down her legs. Then she unfastened the front closure on her bra. "I need you, Farris."

As he tossed the bra aside and moved on top of her,

she felt the dark mourning of the last five years shimmer and disappear in the heat of a new adventure.

"You're mine," he groaned. He moved in her carefully, as if this was their first time.

India curled her legs around his waist, feeling the way he stretched her, filled her. "Always," she whispered. "Don't ever shut me out again."

"I won't," he said, the words husky with emotion.

They both came quickly, their cries mingling as they found release.

India stroked Farris's hair. "I'm sort of regretting the fact that I shipped my engagement ring and wedding ring back to you when we broke up. I guess you had to sell them, too."

He reared up on one elbow, his hair rumpled, his eyes heavy-lidded. He scowled. "I would have chosen to live in a rodent-infested walk-up before doing that. They're in a safety-deposit box at my bank. But to be fair, a second marriage to the same guy probably deserves a bigger ring. As a penalty for my being an ass."

"Don't insult the man I love." She kissed him again, wallowing in the knowledge that tonight was only the beginning.

Her ex-husband, now her fiancé, yawned. "About those zeros…" He teased her nipple, seemingly fascinated with the way it peaked and tightened.

"Hmm?" She was rapidly losing the train of the conversation.

"I'm solid, Inkie, all zeros accounted for. And an extra one for good measure. I got it all back."

"And I got you back," she said. "So the money doesn't matter."

It never did.

Farris laid his head on her breast and sighed. "I love you, India Ink."

"And I love you, cowboy…"

* * * * *

Want more from
USA TODAY *bestselling author Janice Maynard?*

Check out her Men of Stone River trilogy!

After Hours Seduction
Upstairs Downstairs Temptation
Secrets of a Playboy

**WE HOPE YOU ENJOYED
THIS BOOK FROM**

⟨H⟩ HARLEQUIN
DESIRE

*Luxury, scandal, desire—welcome to
the lives of the American elite.*

Be transported to the worlds of oil barons, family dynasties,
moguls and celebrities. Get ready for juicy plot twists,
delicious sensuality and intriguing scandal.

6 NEW BOOKS AVAILABLE EVERY MONTH!

#2851 RANCHER'S FORGOTTEN RIVAL

The Carsons of Lone Rock • by Maisey Yates

No one infuriates Juniper Sohappy more than ranch owner Chance Carson. But when Juniper finds him injured and with amnesia on her property, she must help. He believes he's her ranch hand, and unexpected passion flares. But when the truth comes to light, will everything fall apart?

#2852 FROM FEUDING TO FALLING

Texas Cattleman's Club: Fathers and Sons • by Jules Bennett

When Carson Wentworth wins the TCC presidency, tensions flare between him and rival Lana Langley. But to end their familiy feud and secure a fortune for the club, Carson needs her—as his fake fiancée. If they can only ignore the heat between them...

#2853 A SONG OF SECRETS

Hana Trio • by Jayci Lee

After their breakup a decade ago, cellist Angie Han needs composer Jonathan Shin's song to save her family's organization. Striking an uneasy truce, they find their attraction still sizzles. But as their connection grows, will past secrets ruin everything?

#2854 MIDNIGHT SON

Gambling Men • by Barbara Dunlop

Determined to protect his mentor, ruggedly handsome Alaskan businessman Nathaniel Stone is suspicious of the woman claiming to be his boss's long-lost daughter, Sophie Crush. He agrees to get close to her to uncover her intentions, but he cannot ignore their undeniable attraction...

#2855 MILLION-DOLLAR MIX-UP

The Dunn Brothers • by Jessica Lemmon

With her only client MIA, talent agent Kendall Squire travels to his twin's luxe mountain cabin to ask him to fill in. But Max Dunn left Hollywood behind. Now, as they're trapped by a blizzard, things unexpectedly heat up. Has Kendall found her leading man?

#2856 THE PROBLEM WITH PLAYBOYS

Little Black Book of Secrets • by Karen Booth

Publicist Chloe Burnett is a fixer, and sports agent Parker Sullivan needs her to take down a vicious gossip account. She never mixes business with pleasure, but the playboy's hard to resist. When they find themselves in the account's crosshairs, can their relationship survive?

SPECIAL EXCERPT FROM

HARLEQUIN

DESIRE

*Eve Martin has one goal—find her nephew's father—
and her unlikely ally is hotelier Rafael Wentworth, who's
just returned to Texas and the family who abandoned
him. Soon, she's falling hard for the playboy despite
their differences...and their secrets.*

Read on for a sneak peek at
The Rebel's Return, *by Nadine Gonzalez.*

"I'm opening a guesthouse in town, similar to this, but better."

"You're here to check out the competition, aren't you?"

Rafael raised a finger to his lips. "Shh."

"That's sneaky," Eve said with a little smile. "I knew you had a
motive for coming here."

He winked. "Just not the motive you thought."

She responded with a roll of the eyes. He noticed her long lashes
fanned the high slopes of her cheeks. In the intimate light of the inn's
lobby, her skin was smoother than he could have ever imagined.

Rafael was glad the tension that had built up in the car was
subsiding. He wanted to make her laugh again, the way she'd laughed
when they were alone in the garden. Her laughter had leaped out as
if springing from a sealed cave. He'd wanted to take her in his arms
and hold her close until she settled down.

"Incoming!"

Lost in the fantasy of holding her, he didn't quite understand
what she was saying. "What's that?"

"Just...shut up."

She stepped up to him and brushed her lips to his in a whisper of
a kiss. Rafael tensed, the muscles of his abdomen tightening. "Act
like you're into it," she murmured through clenched teeth. With
every nerve ending in his body setting off sparks, he didn't have to

rely on dormant acting skills. He gripped her waist, pulled her close and kissed her hard, deep and slow. She gripped the lapel of his suit jacket and opened to his kiss. He heard her groan just before she tore herself away.

"I think we're good," she said, her voice shaky.

He was shaken, too. "How the hell do you figure?"

"I kissed you to create a distraction," she said. "P&J just walked in."

Paul and Jennifer Carlton were the most annoying couple in Texas, but at this moment he was making plans to send them a fruit basket and a bottle of wine.

"Here I thought you wanted to test that 'sex in an inn' theory."

"Stop thinking that," she scolded. "They're right over there. Don't look now, though."

He wouldn't dream of it. Her swollen lips had his undivided attention.

"Okay… They've entered the dining hall. You can look now."

"Nah. I'll take your word for it."

The manager returned with the keys to their suite, the one with the two distinct and separate bedrooms. The man was a little red in the face from what he'd undoubtedly witnessed.

Rafael plucked the key cards from his hand. "I'll take those. Thanks."

"Anything else, sir?"

"Send up laundry services, will you?" Rafael said. "And your best bottle of tequila."

The manager cleared his throat. "Certainly, sir. Enjoy your evening."

Don't miss what happens next in
The Rebel's Return *by Nadine Gonzalez,*
the next book in the Texas Cattleman's Club:
Fathers and Sons series!

Available February 2022 wherever
Harlequin Desire books and ebooks are sold.

Harlequin.com

"It's you, isn't it?"

She turned, and there he was.

So close.

Impossibly close.

And she didn't know if she could survive it.

Because those electric blue eyes were looking right into hers. But this time, it wasn't from across a crowded bar. It was right there.

Right there.

And she didn't have a deadweight clinging to her side that kept her from going where she wanted to go, doing what she wanted to do. She was free. Unencumbered, for the first time in fifteen years. For the first damn time.

She was standing there, and she was just Mallory.

Jared wasn't there. Griffin wasn't there. Her parents weren't there.

She was standing on her own, standing there with no one and nothing to tell her what to do, no one and nothing to make her feel a certain thing.

So it was all just him. Blinding electric blue, brilliant and scalding. Perfect.

"I...I think so. Unless...unless you think I'm someone else." It was much less confident and witty than she'd intended. But she didn't feel capable of witty just now.

"You were here once. About six months ago."

He remembered her. He remembered her. This man who had haunted her dreams—no, not haunted, created them—who had filled her mind with erotic imagery that had never existed there before, was…talking about her. He was.

He thought of her. He remembered her.

"I was," she said.

He looked behind her, then back at her. "Where's the boyfriend?"

He asked the question with an edge of hostility. It made her shiver.

"Not here."

"Good." His lips tipped upward into a smile.

"I…" She didn't know what to say. She didn't know what to say because this shimmering feeling inside her was clearly, clearly shared and…

Suddenly her freedom felt terrifying. That freedom that had felt, only a moment before, exhilarating suddenly felt like too much. She wanted to hide. Wanted to scamper under the bar and get behind the bar stool so that she could put something between herself and this electric man. She wondered if she was ready for this.

Because there was no question what this was.

One night.

With nothing at all between them. Nothing but unfamiliar motel bedsheets. A bed she'd never sleep in again and a man she would never sleep with again.

She understood that.

Find out what happens after Mallory and Colt's electrifying night together in
The True Cowboy of Sunset Ridge, *the unmissable final book in Maisey Yates's beloved Gold Valley miniseries!*

Don't miss The True Cowboy of Sunset Ridge
by New York Times bestselling author Maisey Yates, available December 2021 wherever HQN books and ebooks are sold!

HQNBooks.com